THE
HAUNTED MANSION

THE
HAUNTED MANSION

AVA & CAROL DETECTIVE AGENCY

THOMAS LOCKHAVEN
WITH EMILY CHASE

TWISTED KEY
publishing

2018

First Printing: 2018

ISBN 978-1-947744-15-8

Twisted Key Publishing, LLC
405 Waltham Street Suite 116
Lexington, MA 02421

www.twistedkeypublishing.com

Ordering Information:
Special discounts are available on quantity purchases by corporations, associations, educators, and others. For details, contact the publisher at the above listed address.

U.S. trade bookstores and wholesalers: Please contact Twisted Key Publishing, LLC by email twistedkeypublishing@gmail.com.

CONTENTS

I
LIVINGSTON FESTIVITIES ARE HORRIFYING

"Do you want to hear a *real* ghost story?" Ethan Palmer leaned forward, leering at the children who sat huddled in a half-moon around a roaring campfire. The fire cracked and hissed, rebelling against the cold December night.

It was four days before Christmas, and as was Livingston tradition, the kids had spent the afternoon engaged in snowball fights, sledding, and ice skating on Lake Crystal. But now…Ethan Eugene Palmer had decided that the evening of festivities should take on a more sinister tone.

Ethan's face was thin and pale. His green eyes sparkled mischievously in the firelight. He was a few years older than the rest of the kids, and he seemed to take great pleasure in scaring the life out of them.

His unusually red lips curled into an evil grin as he began to spin the tale.

"Everyone here knows the old Butcher house, right?" he asked, jabbing a stick into the fire, sending a fiery cloud of embers skyward. "Well, I found out why it's been empty all these years. You want to know why?"

He paused, looking at each of the children as if daring them to speak.

Finally, a very small voice whispered, "Because it's haunted?"

"No, Riley," smiled Ethan. He shook his head at the group. "At least someone has the courage to speak up. It's something much more evil than your ordinary ghost. Much more evil."

"They're politicians," offered Ava.

"Nice one," whispered Carol.

Ethan glared at the two girls. The usually animated group of children fell silent...as silent as a graveyard.

He rubbed his hands together as if he were about to enjoy an exquisite feast. Then Ethan lowered his voice, and began to speak slowly, mysteriously.

"Most of you have never heard of Jack and Ruby Butcher. But as children, they used to play in their grandparent's house. They had the run of the house, except for their grandmother's room. That room was strictly off limits.

"Their grandma had died, two years earlier...and they say George Butcher, the grandfather, never got over her death." He paused, letting the story settle in.

"One rainy afternoon, while their grandfather was sleeping, Jack and Ruby got bored, and decided to play hide and seek.

"You've all played hide and seek right?" Ethan smiled as the children nodded silently. "Just like you and me…Jack probably placed his hands over his eyes, and softly counted one, two, three, while his sister ran to hide.

"No one knows why…but Ruby decided to sneak up the stairs to her grandmother's bedroom. She didn't want to wake her grandfather, so she took off her shoes, and slowly crept up the stairs.

"She had just reached the top step, when she heard her brother creeping around looking for her.

"Her heart was pounding, she knew that she wasn't supposed to go in her grandma's room…but when she reached for the door knob, the door swung open, all by itself.

"She didn't know what to do, she didn't want to get caught by her grandfather or her brother. So she rushed into her grandmother's room.

"Ruby crept over to the closet and paused. Should she open it? Jack would never look for her there! She pushed her finger down on the latch, and with a metallic click, the door creaked open."

Ethan reached out his hand, pretending to be Ruby reaching for the door.

"When she opened the closet door, the smell of moth balls and stale air hit her like a ton of bricks.

"She was scared," Ethan whispered, "but Jack had just reached the top of the stairs. The closet was tiny, and filled with her grandmother's shoes and clothes…Ruby decided that she would *just* fit.

"She reached in and began to slowly push her grandmother's clothes apart. Suddenly, a bony hand circled around her wrist, squeezing, crushing! Ruby tried to scream, but her throat closed."

Ethan's eyes narrowed evilly. "The skeleton hand began pulling Ruby into the closet!

"'Come, come my sweetie,' a cackling squeaky voice laughed. Ruby's eyes dropped to her wrist…her grandmother's charm bracelet dangled, from the bones.

"Ruby gripped the doorframe with her other hand, but she wasn't strong enough," Ethan said whispering. "Ruby could feel her fingers slipping. Her socked feet slid into the closet. The skeletal arm yanked hard, and Ruby's fingers slipped from the door, clawing at the air…she closed her eyes and fell."

Ethan paused. The children were silent, pressed up against one another, barely breathing. Hanging onto his every word.

"Ruby looked up from the floor. Her brother stood over her, a broken lamp in his hand. A bony finger and their grandmother's charm bracelet lay on the floor at Jack's feet.

"Suddenly the children's grandfather and father rushed into the room. They looked from Jack to Ruby. A purplish black bruise in the shape of a human hand began forming on Ruby's wrist. Jack tried to speak, but the words wouldn't come.

"And then…," said Ethan slowly, "the grandfather turned to the father and smiled… 'you said you liked the little boy the least.' The father nodded…and without speaking, shoved Jack backwards into the closet. Before Ruby could do anything, a skeletal hand wrapped around Jack's waist and pulled him into the closet.

"The very next day, the family disappeared and were never seen again…but they say, Jack's ghost still haunts the Butcher house. That's why it's still empty.

"Ah perfect timing," he smiled at the frightened children as he climbed to his feet. "Your parents are here. Make sure you ask them to drive by the old Butcher house on the way home." He grinned excitedly, waving to the parents as they approached.

Shaken, the children scrambled to their feet and scurried off to the safety of their parents' arms.

"Sleep well!" Ethan called out, obviously pleased with himself. The holidays had officially started.

"That was terrifyingly creepy," whispered Ava as she stood, wiping the snow from the seat of her pants.

"I thought we were gonna sing and roast marshmallows," said Carol, "not give the kids nightmares."

"Your singing gives me nightmares…so I kind of preferred the ghost story," winked Ava.

"You know," smiled Carol, "if we take Whitmore Street, we can walk past the Butcher house on the way home."

Ava made a face, "Really?"

"Ava Clarke," smirked Carol, "what happened to your sense of adventure?"

"It takes a pass when it comes to evil spirits, zombies, me dying in a closet…."

"Come on," said Carol grabbing Ava's hoodie by the sleeve, "it's just an empty old house…what's the worst that could happen?"

2
THE WORST THING HAPPENS

Moonlight fought its way through thick billowy clouds. Streetlights decorated with giant wreaths hung their heads, bathing the snow-covered streets in a pale white light. The girls' snow boots crunched loudly as they traversed Whitmore Street, the home of the Butcher house.

A cold December breeze awakened the trees from their slumber, making a clickity clackety sound that gave Ava the heebie jeebies. She pulled the collar of her puffy purple ski vest up around her neck and grabbed her Santa hat from her vest pocket.

"Woah," said Carol, "Whitmore Street doesn't play around when it comes to decorating."

"It's incredible," agreed Ava, "puts Whoville to shame."

"I can see the Grinch now," laughed Carol, "...forget Whoville, tonight it's Whitmore!"

"Hey, you're stealing my mojo," laughed Ava, "I'm supposed to be the funny one."

"You are the funny one, funny looking," Carol snickered.

The residents of Whitmore Street either forgot that there was a dilapidated old spooky house in the middle of their neighborhood, or they went overboard with Christmas cheer, trying to draw attention away from the house. Everywhere Ava and Carol looked, houses were blanketed in rows of multicolored lights. Golden light shone from windows decorated with electric candles. There were manger scenes, giant candy cane fences, inflatable snowmen and wooden deer made from logs.

Sandwiched in between the holiday cheer...sat an old abandoned house...surrounded by an old, broken down wooden fence.

The girls came to a stop. Somewhere in the distance they could hear a dog barking, otherwise, the night was silent.

"OK," whispered Ava, "we did it, there it is, the Butcher house. Can we go now?"

Carol stood staring at the house. Years of neglect had taken its toll. The wooden shutters that remained, hung precariously from their hinges. The huge steps leading to the front door were broken and sagging. Jagged glass like broken teeth jutted upwards from window frames. But it was the darkness, darker than night, darker than shadow, that seemed to ooze from every window and every door of the Butcher house.

"Yeah...," she paused thinking, "I bet this used to be a beautiful house."

"OK…I think the cold has frozen your brain, let's go. After seeing this neighborhood, I have to reprimand my parents for their lackluster dedication to holiday decoration."

Ava trudged away, already planning additions to their house when Carol whispered excitedly. "A light! I saw a light!"

"What?"

"I saw a light turn on in the house," whispered Carol, "in the basement!"

"You're seeing things. There's no way that house has electricity."

"I know what I saw!" Carol crept closer to the house, crouching behind a small stone column.

The girls stared at the house, waiting, but the house remained dark.

"Maybe it was just a reflection…I mean this neighborhood is lit up like a—"

"It was a light, I saw a light in the basement."

"OK," said Ava holding out her hands, "I believe you!"

Ava's phone buzzed. "Great, it's gonna be my parents wondering where we are."

"OK," acknowledged Carol disappointedly. "I guess we better get going."

The light from Ava's phone illuminated her face while she texted her parents. Carol's eyes scoured every inch of the basement one last time, looking for any hint of light.

"OK," smiled Ava, patting her friend on the back, "my mom's making hot cocoa."

"I love your mom's cocoa," Carol smiled.

The girls walked up the small incline back to Whitmore Street, leaving the Butcher house like a creepy dream behind them.

Ting, Ting...

Crunch. Crunch.

Ting. Ting.

Crunch. Crunch.

Ava paused, "Did you hear a bell?"

Carol stood, breathing quietly, tiny puffs of white smoke escaping her lips. She listened intently.

It was the faintest of sounds. *Ting. Ting.* Like the ringing of a tiny bell. The sound seemed to come from behind them.

Ava couldn't stop herself. It was as if her eyes had a mind of their own. Against her will, she turned and looked at the Butcher house. Carol was right, she could now see a tiny sliver of light in the basement window!

"Carol, I see it," whispered Ava excitedly.

Carol began quickly walking back to the house. "Come on, we've got to get closer."

"Who do you think it is?" whispered Ava. Her eyes scanned the moonlit blanket of snow that surrounded the Butcher house. "There are no footprints."

Carol's eyes quickly scanned the front of the house. "I know," she whispered as she crouched by a crooked pole, supporting what was left of the fence.

Ava hurried over to Carol....

"Shhh," whispered Carol, holding a finger to her lips.

"Sorry, the snow is really crunchy."

The light grew brighter for a second, and then only a sliver remained. Something or someone was definitely there.

Ava's heart quickened. Inside her head, curiosity battled common sense. "We should crawl to the window," suggested Ava, "that way we won't make as much noise."

"Good idea," Carol paused....

Ava felt a chill along the back of her neck.

A shadow had fallen over them.... They could see two furry arms, and a body...with no head.

The girls turned their heads in unison, standing over them, was a headless creature! It had an elongated fury torso, and thin sinewy arms that ended in enormous clawed fingers. Where the head was supposed to be, there was only a thick stump of a neck.

The girls screamed in terror, as the creature swiped at Ava, its claws just missing her face! She fell backwards, hard onto the snow. She backpedaled on the slippery crusty ice like a crab. The creature lunged at Carol as she dove headfirst into an icy snow bank.

The creature reached down grabbing Carol's candy cane striped hoodie, lifting her off the ground! Ava grabbed a board from the fence, and struck the creature hard on the back. The creature stumbled, dropping Carol, whirling on Ava!

"Run!" screamed Carol.

Ava didn't need to be told twice, the girls ran slipping and sliding toward the street, the monster right on their heels!

3
TRAPPED

Ava and Carol raced down Whitmore Street. Carol motioned to her right, and Ava followed her through a yard decorated like Santa's workshop. Inside the house, a dog began jumping up and down at the front window, barking ferociously.

Ava looked over her shoulder, the headless creature was closing in! The girls scrambled through the backyard, into a small cluster of woods. They each stood silently behind trees, trying to calm their breathing.

They could hear its footsteps, the slow crunch, crunch in the snow, getting closer. Carol swallowed hard. What was going on?!

Ava was staring at her wide-eyed…trembling.

The woods had gone silent. The girls strained their ears listening. Nothing.

Carol ever so slowly peeked around the tree. There was nothing but shadows. She slowly exhaled. Then suddenly, she was yanked against the tree, the bark digging into her cheek as stars exploded in her head! Snow showered down on her and the creature. She wrenched her hand backwards, twisting and turning, until her mitten came off, freeing her hand. The monster threw it to the ground, and the girls were off, running for their lives!

"Follow me!" yelled Ava.

Carol and Ava sprinted through the woods, and down a narrow path. They hurdled a small chain hanging between two wooden posts. Less than thirty minutes had passed since the girls had sat here at Lake Crystal, listening to Ethan Palmer's horror story...and now the girls were living it!

The girls breathed heavily, the cold air burning their lungs, smoke pouring from their mouths like steam engines. They crossed the shore, and then Ava leapt onto the icy lake and slid expertly. Carol did the same, leaping onto the ice she crouched and slid like a snowboarder. The monster hesitated for a moment, and then dashed onto the ice, only to come crashing down on its back.

The girls didn't waste a second, they pushed off with their heels, using their boots like ice skates. Within moments, they had crossed the frozen lake and jumped down, into a cluster of icy boulders that covered a steep slope.

The girls huddled behind a huge rock, hoping the monster would give up. Looking around, Ava realized they had made a mistake. They had trapped themselves between two huge boulders, with only one way out.

Carol looked at Ava, her crystal blue eyes filled with fear.

"Don't worry," whispered Ava, "we got this!"

She stared at the opening between the two rocks—a miniature avalanche of smaller rocks, slid down the hill directly behind them. Ava's fingers clawed at the snow-covered ground, looking for anything she could use as a weapon. Her fingers circled around a cold stone, the size of a golf ball. *Perfect!*

Crunch. Crunch. The footsteps grew closer. Carol was sure the monster could hear her heart pounding against her chest. A dark shadow slowly slid over the rock where the girls hid. Carol pressed back hard against Ava…they were trapped! Ava squeezed the rock hard, it was going to be her only chance.

"Boo!!!!!"

Ava jumped up screaming "*Yaaaaaaa!*" like a wild woman and hurled the rock at the beast….

Except, it wasn't the beast, it was Kevin Chen…one of the older neighborhood kids.

Ava watched horrified as the rock flew like a missile and hit Kevin in the chest with a loud thwack!

"Owwwww!" he said placing his hand on his chest.

"I'm so sorry Kevin! I thought you were…."

Carol slammed her hand over Ava's mouth. "She thought you were a bear. You know, lots of bears this time of year. Can never be too careful."

Kevin arched an eyebrow, then nodded, "…Yeah my bad, sorry I scared you guys."

"Sorry I almost shattered your sternum," said Ava.

"Oh that," laughed Kevin, "it was nothing, don't worry, I barely felt it."

"What?!" asked Ava insulted. "I mean yeah, my foot slipped on some ice when I went to throw it. Normally I can pretty much hurl a rock over a mile."

Carol raised her eyebrows and smiled at Kevin. "She's been known to exaggerate just a little."

"Hey, George Washington threw a rock across the Rappahannock River...and no one doubted him...so show a little respect."

"OK," laughed Kevin holding up his hands in surrender. "We believe you!"

"What's that?" asked Carol pointing to a small rectangular object in Kevin's hand.

"It's a motion capture camera. I was grabbing it when I saw you guys run behind the boulder."

Carol's eyes flickered over to the boulder where they had been hiding just moments ago, and then up the small hill to the edge of the lake. *Kevin must have scared the creature off.*

"Why do you have a motion capture camera in the woods?" asked Carol.

"I actually have several set up. There's all kinds of wildlife out there."

You're telling me, thought Carol.

"Oh cool, my dad has one of those," replied Ava, "have you seen anything interesting?"

"Sure," said Kevin, "coyotes, fox, wild turkey and a beaver family. You'll have to come over and check out the pictures some time!"

"Oh wow, thanks," said Carol, "that would be awesome."

Ava's phone vibrated. She reached into her pocket and stared at the screen, her head dropped. "Oh boy," she moaned, "I'm in so much trouble."

"Don't worry," said Carol putting her arm around Ava's shoulders. "I'll be your backup."

Ava smiled. "Come on Kevin, walk with us. You can tell us more about the wild beasts that lurk in our forest."

"You would be surprised!"

Ava and Carol looked at each other and smiled…. *You wanna bet?* thought Carol, *you wanna bet?*

The trio climbed up the hill to the lake, slipping and sliding their way to the other side. No one noticed the headless monster, hidden in the trees, watching them from the shadows.

4
HOODWINKED

"Good morning, and ouch!" said Ava, checking out Carol's scraped and swollen cheek. "That looks like it hurts."

Carol smiled, "It looks worse than it feels."

"In that case, mind if I thump it?" asked Ava a little too eagerly.

"What? What kind of question is that? Of course, I mind. Someone needs to check your Netflix browsing history; I'm worried about you."

"Awe," said Ava, bumping her shoulder into Carol, "someone cares."

"Give me strength," whispered Carol, gazing skyward.

"Did your parents ask about your face?"

"Yeah, I told my parents that my sled and I had a brief collision with some shrubbery."

"Good thinking!"

"I thought so too," replied Carol.

"Too bad it wasn't mistletoe; you could have crashed and gotten a sympathy kiss from Noah Riley, a.k.a secret crush." Ava made the shape of a heart on her chest with her two hands.

"I'd rather kiss a frog," said Carol, shaking her head.

"That can be arranged," laughed Ava.

The girls walked quietly for a moment, taking in the scenery. It felt good to laugh. A blanket of snow covered Livingston. Overnight, the road crew had done their job. The sidewalks had been shoveled and the streets cleared.

Carol loved walking down Main Street at Christmastime. Livingston did Christmas right. Street corners were adorned with beautiful old street lights, wrapped in garland and red ribbons. Storefronts glistened with displays decorated with Christmas trees and wreaths. Classical music played old holiday classics. Everyone seemed happier, kinder.

Ava took in a deep breath; the aroma of pumpkin spice coffee and hot apple cider filled the air. The girls stopped and purchased two cups of hot chocolate and then continued toward the center of town.

"I was thinking about last night," said Carol suddenly. "I think that it was Ethan…or one of his friends. Think about it. He tells a scary story…"

"…and he practically dares us to go by the Butcher house," added Ava, seeing where Carol was going.

"Exactly. And when we do…," nodded Carol, "…a headless monster suddenly appears and chases us. It just seems a little suspicious to me."

Disappointment filled Ava's face; she was hoping they had a new mystery to uncover.

"Plus, there's this," said Carol, handing her phone to Ava.

Ava tilted the phone so she could see it in the bright sunlight. "That jerk! You mean to tell me I was frightened to death by a cheap $49 synthetic-fur costume from Amazon?!"

"We both were.... He's probably got Amazon Prime," winked Carol.

"So witty...but really, it doesn't make sense," said Ava, shaking her head.

"You're right," replied Carol, pointing. "Look!"

Ava turned, following Carol's gesture. Just ahead of them, yellow police tape was stretched across the sidewalk and the entrance to the Charter Bank.

The girls recognized Mr. Charter as he stood and talked with three uniformed police officers and a man dressed in a gray suit and black trench coat. Behind them were two Livingston police cars and a black SUV with the letters "FBI" on the side. A crowd of people had gathered on the sidewalk, talking excitedly.

"Whoa!" exclaimed Ava. "That doesn't look good."

"Not at all," replied Carol. "It must've been a robbery."

The Charter Bank was the oldest bank in Livingston, dating back to 1806. The bank had been passed down through generations of Charters.

Ava stood shaking her head. "Why would anyone rob a bank right before Christmas? Not only is that completely uncool…it's just evil."

Carol was about to reply when she felt a tug on her sleeve. She looked behind her into the eyes of a blond-haired boy wearing a black hoodie and jeans.

"Derik," she whispered.

"Derik?" asked Ava, quickly turning.

He quickly put his finger to his lips and then looked around, making sure no one had noticed him.

"Derik, what's going on? Are you okay?" asked Carol.

"Yes and no," he replied. "Follow me. I can't talk here."

The trio quickly skirted around the crowd and then ducked under the yellow police tape. A uniformed officer who looked like a bulldozer with a buzz cut immediately stopped them, blocking their path with his immense body.

"Holy moly," whispered Ava.

"I'm sorry," he said dryly. "Charter Bank is closed today."

Derik Charter pulled the hood from his head. The officer immediately recognized him, replacing his stern look with a tight smile.

"Morning, Mr. Charter."

"Morning, Officer Tiny," said Derik.

"And these are—" he prompted, motioning to the girls, obviously not happy with them being there.

"*Close* family friends," said Derik.

The officer hesitated, obviously not pleased with the situation, but nevertheless he stepped aside.

"Here," said Ava, handing the officer her hot chocolate. "I just bought it, and I haven't drunk from it. You look like you could use it more than me."

The officer shifted his immense frame and stared at the steaming cup of hot chocolate. A tendril of smoke wafted up to his nose.

"Thank you," he replied gruffly.

"You're welcome," replied Ava, giving him a massive toothy smile.

The first thing that hit the girls was the acrid smell that filled the lobby. It reminded Ava of the time she was seven years old and had jabbed a fork into the electrical outlet—zap, sparks, and smoke—and then the lights went out.

It also reminded her that she had blamed Carol for the fork incident.

"Sorry," whispered Ava.

"What?" asked Carol.

"There's a reason why my parents only allowed you to use plastic forks at my house…until last year. I'll explain later."

Carol gave Ava the all-too-familiar *you're a strange human being* look and then turned her attention to Derik. "What exactly happened?" asked Carol, looking around the bank lobby.

"Someone broke into the bank last night—we're not exactly sure when or how—and stole nearly half a million dollars."

"A half a million dollars?!" gasped Ava.

"I'm terribly sorry, Derik," said Carol, shaking her head. *A half million dollars....* She could barely comprehend that much money. "What will your dad do?"

"He's going to do everything that he can do to catch the thieves."

The girls looked up as Mr. Charter walked into the bank lobby. He was elegantly dressed, his hair combed into a perfect part. You would never have known that he had been up all night.

"Mr. Charter," said Carol, "we're so sorry about the robbery."

"Thank you, girls. I never thought that it would happen. Nearly two hundred years in Livingston…this is the first time Charter Bank has been robbed," he shook his head sadly.

"Dad," began Derik, somewhat unsure how to proceed, "Ava and Carol just got back from Italy—they actually helped recover an extremely valuable artifact that was stolen…and they helped the police right here."

"I know," smiled Mr. Charter politely, holding up his hands. "They solved the museum robbery and helped the police catch a group of smugglers."

"So, I just thought…it wouldn't hurt to have them look around," prodded Derik gently.

"That's up to them," Mr. Charter's eyes narrowed. "Do you want to see if the investigators missed anything?"

Ava set her jaw and placed her hands on her hips. "Count us in."

The girls followed Mr. Charter through a row of offices, down a narrow hallway to the back of the bank. At the end of the hallway there was a huge imposing gate made of titanium bars blocking the entrance to the room that housed the safe. The gate made a huge clunking noise as Mr. Charter unlocked it.

In the center of the room stood an enormous vault. The girls stared unbelieving at the eighteen-inch hole burned through the wall of the safe.

"Carol, look!" gasped Ava, pointing at the hole in the safe.

"The FBI believes they used a tool called a plasma cutter," said Mr. Charter.

"A plasma cutter? Sounds like a sci-fi weapon!" exclaimed Ava.

"Yes, it does," Mr. Charter nodded. "Unfortunately, this sci-fi weapon cut a gaping eighteen-inch hole through six inches of layered steel."

"How did they get all of that equipment in here without anyone noticing?" asked Carol.

"Well…that's the thing. Plasma cutters come in a portable unit that looks like an oversized toolbox. They are quite portable."

"Oh," replied Carol as she walked over to the safe. The door was open, revealing an upended money cart, huge bags of coins, and walls of safety deposit boxes.

"What *exactly* did they take?" asked Carol. "I mean, the safe deposit boxes aren't damaged, and there's still a lot of stuff in here."

"Cash," answered Mr. Charter. "We had a lot of extra cash for Christmas…. They picked the perfect time of year to rob us."

"Smart," whispered Carol. "The coin bags would have been too bulky, and breaking into the safe deposit boxes could take a lot of time."

Ava's eyes roamed around the interior of the room. "How did they get in?"

"We have no idea. The doors and windows were locked from the inside. The titanium door was still locked and armed, and the alarm was never triggered."

"What about the ventilation system?" asked Ava, pointing to the ceiling. Directly above the safe was a small rectangular vent about the size of a shoebox.

Mr. Charter shook his head. "Agents searched the roof; there were no footprints, and the ventilation system hadn't been tampered with. Plus...," he paused, thinking, "...a child couldn't fit through that system."

"What about the security video?" asked Carol, pointing to a camera mounted in the corner.

"Nothing. The thieves stole the hard drive and cut the internet cable, so there was no backup to the online server."

Ava shook her head, "It's like they teleported here."

"It was well planned," acknowledged Mr. Charter.

"Nothing on the traffic cams or store cams?" asked Carol.

"The police are going through store video and street cams, but these guys are professionals. They aren't hopeful."

"Do you mind if we take some pictures?" asked Carol. "We promise to keep them private."

Mr. Charter hesitated, "Go ahead. I have to replace this old safe anyway. It's nearly 160 years old." He placed his hand on the side of the old safe.

Carol looked at him. She was sure his mind was flooded with memories.

Ava and Carol spent about twenty minutes taking pictures of the vault, ceiling, walls, windows, doors, and floor.

Ava asked Mr. Charter, "Did anyone take a picture of the crowd?"

"No…why?" asked Mr. Charter.

"Because many times suspects come back to the scene of the crime as a part of the crowd. That way they can observe the investigation."

"Sounds risky. I mean, coming back to a place you just robbed," said Mr. Charter.

"They are usually in disguise…but you never know."

"I'll ask Lieutenant Norris," Mr. Charter clasped his hand and exhaled.

The girls recognized this all-too-familiar pattern of body language as: *It's time to finish up here.*

"Well, I think that we've got enough to go on for now," said Carol, smiling. "We'll let you know right away if we come up with anything."

"Thank you," smiled Mr. Charter. He led the girls through the hallway back to the lobby. "Thank you again, Ava. Thank you, Carol," he said, smiling at both girls. "Let me know if you find anything."

"We will," the girls chorused.

Derik walked with the girls onto the front steps of the bank. "Thank you for taking the time to look around…it was really cool of you."

"We'll make this case our top priority," said Ava seriously.

"Thank you," Derik smiled. "You guys are awesome. Do you really think you can solve it? I mean…these guys are pros."

"Yeah, but they're human," replied Carol with a smile. "And humans make mistakes…. It's just like my grandma used to say: 'It only takes one lose thread to unravel a blanket.'"

"I like that," said Derik. He stared at Carol for a moment. "Can I add my number to your phone?"

"Sure!" Carol unlocked her phone and handed it to Derik.

"Be sure to share it with Ava," he smiled as he typed in the digits.

The girls said their goodbyes, their minds filled with their new mystery…oblivious to the tiny black drone that hovered high above the bank, watching them.

5
THE LAIR

"We actually have two mysteries," said Ava as she grabbed a piping-hot sausage pizza from the microwave.

The girls had turned Ava's basement into a crime-solving think tank called The Lair. Using some of the award money from the Hancock Museum of Archeology, the girls had created a state-of-the-art crime lab.

A laptop and printer sat perched on a desk at one end of the room, with an old couch in the middle of the room that faced a huge, stand-alone magnetic whiteboard. The far end of the room had a small kitchenette, and behind the whiteboard on the back wall was a table with a microscope and chemistry set—a gift from Ava's dad, a prominent biologist.

Carol was hunched over the laptop. A moment later, the printer began whirring. "Here they come," said Carol. "The pictures we took at the bank. So, what were you saying about two mysteries?"

"Well, before our walk yesterday was rudely interrupted by the bank robbery, you said that you thought the headless monster was Ethan or one of his friends."

"Yes…," recalled Carol.

"Well, we know that Ethan can be immature, but in the end, he would never do anything to actually *hurt* us. Think about it, whoever was dressed up as the headless monster…the way he grabbed at us, the way he yanked your beautiful face into the tree…and then kept chasing us…. Ethan would have never done that."

Carol nodded, "Yeah, you're right." The thought actually made her shudder. "So, who do you think it is?"

"I'm not sure," said Ava. "All of this seems strange. The Butcher house…and then the bank."

"Do you think they are connected?"

"Your guess is as good as mine, but I have an idea that might help us find out."

"I'm all ears," said Carol. "Fire away."

"I'll be right back."

Ava disappeared through the doorway and up the stairs, while Carol attached the pictures from the bank onto the whiteboard. She dated the pictures and then wrote a brief description beneath each one.

On the far right of the board she wrote the word "Suspects" and underlined it twice. She stood staring at the whiteboard. They really didn't have *any* suspects. Ava popped into the room holding a camouflaged, rectangular device with an antenna.

"I'm afraid to ask," said Carol, eyeing the device in Ava's hand.

"This," began Ava proudly, "is a wireless trail camera. Remember Kevin had them to watch woodland creatures? Dad uses his for work."

"Cool...and this is gonna help us *how*?"

"This bad boy has a motion detector and can see in the dark. If there is any type of movement, it will snap a picture. It also has a live video feed. Meaning we can eat pizza and spy on the Butcher house at the same time."

"And you plan on putting this...?"

"We plan on putting this on a tree, facing the Butcher house. If there's anything suspicious going on, we'll see it. Safe in our secret hideout."

"I'm impressed," said Carol, smiling. "You keep coming up with ideas like that, and I may keep you on the payroll."

6
OPERATION NIGHT STALKER

The moon shone so brightly it looked like a train barreling down from the heavens toward the girls. As Ava and Carol walked down the sidewalk, Ava could see the lights from TVs glowing from living rooms and families in kitchens preparing for dinner.

Ava had grabbed her dad's Thor 2000 flashlight in case the headless guy appeared again. The Thor 2000 would temporarily blind anyone who was unfortunate enough to be on its receiving end—which seemed like a brilliant idea at first, but then she remembered he was headless and didn't have eyes.

The girls paused when they reached Whitmore Street. In the distance, they could see the Butcher house. Carol shivered, her finger unconsciously touching the bruise on her cheek.

"Okay," said Ava, "we need to find a tree within one hundred feet of the house that gives us the view we need."

Carol's eyes traveled from the house to a small clump of trees. It was perfect; the trees stood on a small hill that looked directly down toward the house. "Right there," said Carol, pointing. "It's our best vantage spot."

"All right," said Ava, "let's do this."

The girls ran between two houses, clambered over a fence, and then crouch-ran to the cluster of trees. They sat quietly in the shadows, listening for any movement. Carol unzipped her jacket and pulled out a pair of binoculars.

Carol stared through her binoculars at the house for what seemed like an eternity.

"Well," prompted Ava, "see anything?"

"Nothing. It's completely dark."

"Okay," whispered Ava, "I'm gonna set up the camera."

Carol nodded, "I'll keep an eye out."

Ava crawled on her hands and knees to the front of the cluster of trees. She sat with her back to the tree as she unzipped her backpack and pulled out the camera. The camera had small straps that allowed her to secure it to the tree. Ava switched the camera to the "on" position, waited for the green light to come on, and then crawled back to Carol.

Ava crouched beside Carol and pulled out her phone. She typed in the IP address assigned to the camera into her browser, and instantly the Butcher house came into view.

"Whoa!" whispered Carol. "That is freaking awesome! It's, like, perfectly clear."

"I know," whispered Ava. "I had no idea it would work this well." She was afraid that it would turn out to be a grainy disappointment, but the image was clear and crisp. "Let's get back to The Lair before my parents realize we are missing."

Video surveillance turned out to be incredibly boring. Carol had hooked an HDMI cable from the laptop to their TV so they could watch the house, but aside from the occasional car, or neighbor walking a dog, nothing out of the ordinary happened.

Ava jolted awake. *What was that?* she thought, sitting upright on the couch. She and Carol had fallen asleep on the couch watching the Butcher house. A half-filled bag of microwave popcorn had spilled over them. Ava's reaction startled Carol awake as well, and her eyes froze on the TV.

"Ava, look!" said Carol, jabbing her index finger toward the screen.

Ava's eyes grew wide—the headless monster had their camera. The girls watched in horror as the camera rotated, and they saw themselves on the television screen. They jumped from the sofa and looked around the room, confused.

"How are we on the—"

"There!" screamed Carol, pointing to the window at the back of the room.

Ava clawed at the light switch. "Get down!" she whispered.

Ava and Carol crawled to the other side of the couch. They could see the dark shadow of the headless man outside the window. Suddenly a chilling voice came from the TV, filling the room.

"This is your last warning," it growled. "Accidents do happen."

There was a thud as the creature dropped the camera. The girls stared at the TV as the camera slowly sank into the snow. They listened to the crunching of his footsteps as he disappeared into the darkness.

"I really, really do not like that guy," Ava muttered.

Carol shook her head, still trembling. "At least he brought back the camera."

7
DIAMONDS

Ava threw a vicious front kick and then a hook, followed by an uppercut. Her opponent's eyes narrowed, her mouth sneering.

"Oh, you think you can handle this?" Ava growled.

Carol shook her head. "Are you fighting yourself again?"

Ava stared back at herself in the mirror. "Someone's got to protect us." She threw another flurry of punches and kicks.

"I think I'll choose the girl in the mirror," said Carol.

"Me?" asked Ava happily.

"No, not you. Your reflection."

Ava was about to retaliate when Carol's phone chimed. A second later, Ava's phone vibrated too.

"It's Derik," said Carol, looking up from her phone. "Key's Jewelers was robbed last night!"

"Key's Jewelers?!" Ava exclaimed. "What the heck?"

"Texting Derik now," replied Carol.

Ava waited impatiently as Carol's fingers flew across the screen. Moments later, her phone buzzed.

"Oh, cool," said Carol, reading. "His dad is good friends with the manager of Key's Jewelers. He said he's got something important to tell us. Is it okay if Derik comes over?" asked Carol.

"Of course! I'll let my mom know he's coming."

***

"Wow," whispered Derik, turning in a circle, taking in the room. "This is where you solve your crimes?"

"It is," smiled Ava. "Its official name is *The Lair*."

"The Lair," he repeated. "I like it." Derik walked over to the whiteboard. "These are the pictures you took from our bank. Have you found any clues yet?"

"Not yet," said Carol. "We've really just started to piece things together."

"I'm sure we will," added Ava quickly, seeing the disappointment on Derik's face.

"Derik, what was it that you wanted to tell us about the jewelry robbery?" asked Carol.

"Oh, yeah. Well, my dad is good friends with Tracy Morris…."

The girls looked at him expectantly. "Sorry, Derik, we have no idea who that is," admitted Carol.

"Tracy is the owner of Key's Jewelers. She stopped by the house this morning to speak to my dad about the robbery. I wasn't really supposed to hear their conversation…but—"

"But you did?" asked Ava excitedly.

"I did," he nodded. "it was like déjà vu. The thieves broke in and cut open their safe…and took all of their cash and diamonds."

"Oh," said Ava. "I thought they locked the diamonds in those little display tables."

"They keep some of the less expensive pieces in the displays, but their cash and most valuable pieces are locked in the safe at night."

"Out of sight, out of mind," said Carol.

"Exactly. Tracy said she went in early this morning to get ready for their big Christmas sale when she realized the store had been robbed."

"Let me guess," said Carol, "no alarm, no video, doors and windows still locked."

"Yep…my dad asked her the same questions."

"You don't suppose these are inside jobs do you?" asked Ava. "I mean, employees would have the alarm codes."

"Their alarm system works pretty much like the one at our bank. To disable the alarm, you have to type in a passcode. Each time the passcode is entered, it records the date and time."

"And I'm guessing that no one entered the code?" asked Carol.

"Nope. When the police checked, the alarm was armed at 7:00 p.m. when she left work. It wasn't accessed again until 7:00 a.m. the next morning."

"How do you get into a locked room without triggering an alarm and then vanish?" wondered Ava out loud.

"Not only get in, but get in and out with a plasma cutter, bags of cash…and diamonds," added Derik.

Carol walked around the room, tapping her head. Something was right there on the edge of her brain, just out of reach.

"Carol," shouted Ava, "look at the video!"

"Is that the Butcher house?" asked Derik.

Carol nodded, eyes glued to the screen. A laser-thin line of light shone through one of the windows.

"Did you see it?!" Ava quickly reset the video from the night before back thirty seconds. Two seconds later, the light appeared.

"Wait, why do you have a video of the Butcher house…and why is there a light inside?"

"Do you remember Ethan's story about the house being haunted?" Carol asked.

"Yeah…," said Derik.

"Well, Ava and I decided to kind of check it out for ourselves."

Derik smiled. "I should have known you two would—"

He froze, staring at the TV. Suddenly, the video camera was ripped from the tree. It arched skyward for a second and then the video went dead. The trio stood silently staring at the screen.

"Well, that was violent," whispered Derik.

Ava and Carol nodded. Suddenly, the video feed began playing again.

The video jostled and jumped—but one thing became clear.

"It's the back of my house," said Ava.

A headless shadow loomed on the outside of the house, and then there they were, Ava and Carol asleep on the couch.

Ava watched herself bolt upright on the couch; she could see her mouth moving, her breath caught in her throat.

Then the creature's voice filled the room. "This is your last warning," it growled. "Accidents do happen."

The monster dropped the camera, and the screen was filled with icy static as the camera sank into the snow.

A chill raced up Carol's spine as she and Ava looked at each other.

"*What* just happened?" asked Derik. "What was that?"

"That headless thing is what chased us a couple nights ago," said Carol. "It wants us to stay away from the Butcher house."

"The video was from a trail camera we set up in the woods near the house. It has a live video feed, so we thought we could safely monitor the house from The Lair. Obviously I didn't do a great job of hiding the camera," added Ava.

"So, you are telling me that a monster chased you from the Butcher house?!" Derik yelled.

"No," said Carol. "I'm telling you that someone *dressed* like a headless monster chased us."

"The fact that he knows where we live makes things a little more…unnerving," added Ava.

"That video was mega creepy," said Derik.

"Oh yeah, my dad's camera." Ava poked her head outside. "It's snowing hard."

Carol grabbed her boots and jacket. "Awesome! I'll go out with you. I want to see if our headless friend left any tracks."

"Like snow boot tracks," laughed Derik, "or big furry ones?"

"I'm betting on size twelve snow boots," replied Carol.

The trio trudged along the back of the house to the window where the headless monster had watched them the night before. There were only slight indentations left in the snow; the heavy snowfall had pretty much covered the monster's footprints.

Carol knelt and ever so gently began to brush away the new fluffy snow that had fallen and covered the tracks. "It's too hard to tell what's what…. And if the snow keeps falling like this, you won't even be able to tell he was even here."

41

"Yep," replied Ava. She was on her knees digging through the snow, looking for her dad's camera. Derik dropped down to his knees to help.

"If you didn't know your dad's camera was under here, you wouldn't find it until spring," said Derik, scooping through the snow.

Carol froze in place.... Suddenly, everything clicked.

"Guys, I think I know how they broke in! Come on!"

8
CAN YOU DIG IT?

"Where *exactly* are we going?" asked Ava as they trudged through the snow.

"To the one place that can prove my theory right! The Livingston Public Works Department."

"Sounds fascinating," moaned Ava. "How come your clues never take us to say...the mall? Starbucks?"

The Public Works Department was located on Bell Street about a quarter of a mile from the center of town. The streets were filled with laughing and chattering holiday shoppers and tourists, colorful bags swinging from their arms. The trio paused in front of Key's Jewelers. Ava's heart felt a sudden pang of sadness. Inside she could see sparsely filled display cases—and there was Tracy Morris inside, sipping her coffee, looking utterly lost.

Ava turned toward her friends; she could tell by their somber expressions that Derik and Carol saw Tracy too. In a time when Livingston was usually filled with holiday cheer and excitement, an evil menace seemed determined to ruin Christmas for everyone.

"We're gonna catch whoever did this," said Ava. She pulled her hand from her glove and touched the window, feeling the cold glass. In her heart of hearts, she knew that they were going to make this right.

"Okay," said Carol, "we need to get moving. I'm not sure how late Public Works is open today."

Per Derik's suggestion the trio made one more quick stop. They grabbed three steaming hot decaf mochas and then continued their journey.

"This is perfect sledding snow," said Derik as they crossed the railroad tracks.

"Yeah," said Carol, agreeing distractedly. Right now, sledding was the last thing she was interested in.

"Where is this place?" groaned Ava. "I can no longer feel my face."

"Right there," said Derik, pointing. "It's the only brick building...well...besides the post office and the dentist office. Oh, and that new lawyer's office. Never mind. It's that brick building with the dark-green shutters."

A man with a scruffy beard wearing a Livingston Tigers football jersey was shoveling the sidewalk leading up to the public works building. He stepped aside and leaned on his shovel, giving the trio a curious stare as they passed by.

"Cah-ful on those steps," he called out in a thick Bostonian accent. "They're wicked slippery."

"Thank you!" Derik yelled back.

The man wasn't kidding. Even though the steps were covered in rock salt, the steps were still treacherous.

"If I fall to my death," began Ava as they ascended the stairs, "you can have my shoes."

"So gracious," said Carol.

"I wasn't talking to you," smiled Ava.

"I'll treasure them forever," said Derik, laughing.

Stale, warm air greeted the trio as they stepped into the lobby. The walls were painted a pale blue and were covered with paintings and photographs of Livingston and historically notable Livingstonians. Tiny speakers festooned in the corners of the room played an ancient version of "Silent Night."

"Frank Sinatra," whispered Derik.

"Where?" asked Ava.

"The music. The man singing is Frank Sinatra."

"Oh, cool. I like his voice. Is he in a group?"

"Yes," answered Carol. "The Backstreet Boys. Focus, Ava."

"Sorry...."

The trio approached a massive oak desk that stretched across the center of the room. Behind the desk they could see a series of hallways illuminated by flickering fluorescent lights.

"This place is in need of some serious interior decorating," whispered Ava. She looked at Carol and Derik. "I don't see anyone. Should I?" she asked, pointing at a small brass bell that sat on the desk.

"Go for it," said Derik.

Ava smacked the bell twice with the palm of her hand. "Whoa, that was a lot louder than I thought it was going to be."

From somewhere in the back of the building, they heard shuffling, a door slam, and then hurried footsteps.

"Well. Hello, hello, hello." A thin man with a goatee and ponytail appeared behind the desk. Ava cringed as he wiped his nose on his sleeve and then interlaced his fingers, cracking his knuckles.

"Hi, Mr. Cooper," said Carol.

"Good afternoon...and do I know you?" he asked, narrowing his eyes.

"Your nametag," smiled Carol, pointing to a black tag with white lettering that read *H. Cooper.*

"Oh yes, yes," his hand flew up to the tag. "I always forget about that thing. So, how can I help you?"

Derik and Ava turned to Carol. This was her big moment.

"I was visiting the Livingston government website—"

"She doesn't get out much," said Ava.

Carol turned, giving Ava the angry-eyes look.

"Sorry," said Ava, "please continue."

"The site said that you archive all of the maps of the city here. Many dating back to when Livingston was first settled."

"Yes, we do," said Mr. Cooper, his face filling with pride.

"Awesome! Mr. Cooper, we're looking for—"

"Please call me Harvey."

"Okay, um, Harvey…I'm looking for a specific map, one that shows the underground tunnel system below Livingston."

Ava noticed Harvey grip the edge of his desk a little tighter.

Carol pulled her phone from her coat, and after a series of swipes, she turned the screen to Harvey.

"The website said that this map is here. The one that shows the entire tunnel system. Do you have it?"

"Why are you interested in the tunnel system? Most of it collapsed and was filled in nearly one hundred years ago."

Carol was caught off guard by Harvey's reaction.

"We're working on a historical painting of Livingston for our history class," said Derik, jumping in. "We're painting a panoramic of the city from the 1800s, the 1900s, and present time. We just wanted an accurate representation and thought showing the tunnels would be a cool addition."

47

"Most of my classmates have no idea that they even exist," offered Ava.

"Yes, yes, I suppose most people don't," Harvey replied. "Give me just a second."

"Whoa," said Carol softly as Harvey disappeared down the hallway. "Good job!"

"Captain of the debate team," smiled Derik. "Gotta be quick on my feet."

"I've got really quick feet," said Ava. "They just don't connect to my brain like yours."

"Here we go...," said Harvey as he carefully laid out an aerial picture of the entire city. The picture was about four feet wide and two feet tall. It was composed of what looked like a series of individual photos that had been stitched together.

"I'm confused," said Carol, studying the photo. "Where are the tunnels?"

"Oh, right here," said Harvey, pointing at the map. "These dark gray lines underneath the buildings represent the tunnel system. See, here's the old church, and right here is the town hall. This is Main Street," he said, tracing his finger along the map.

"That's Main Street?" asked Ava.

"Yes, there's the Main Street Diner. See how the tunnel system went right under the Baptist church? They used the tunnel to smuggle food and supplies."

"And you're sure this is accurate?" asked Carol.

"Oh yes, this is the official government map for Livingston…you can see the date and government seal right here."

Carol's shoulders slumped. "Do you mind if I take a picture for us to use…you know…for our project?"

"Oh, certainly," smiled Harvey. "Take as many as you like."

"Thanks," mumbled Carol as she zoomed in on the map and took several photos.

"Well," said Harvey, folding his hands together. "I'm about to close up shop. Anything else I can help you with?"

"No, sir," said Carol.

"Harvey. Just call me Harvey. 'Sir' makes me feel old."

"Thank you, Harvey," said Carol. "You've been a big help."

"You're welcome," he smiled. "Merry Christmas."

"Merry Christmas," said the group as they walked to the door.

"So," said Derik as they paused on the top of the steps. "You thought the bad guys used the tunnel system."

"Yeah," sighed Carol, clearly upset. "I thought I'd figured it out."

"It would have made sense," said Ava.

"But according to that map, from what I could tell, the tunnel never ran beneath your dad's bank or the jewelry store. Sorry, guys."

"It's okay," said Ava, resting her head on Carol's shoulder. "We'll figure it out."

9
DIVE BOMBER

"I'm dead," cried Derik, jumping up from his seat.

"What is it?" asked Carol.

"My parents' Christmas party is tonight!" gasped Derik. "I was supposed to help get the house ready. Ugh!"

He yanked his coat from the back of his chair, knocking it loudly to the floor.

"Derik," said Ava, picking up the chair and helping him with his coat. "Give your dad a call—tell him you're on your way."

He gave Ava an *are you kidding me* look.

She countered with, "Trust me on this one. You have no idea what we've put our parents through."

Derik hesitated. Darkness had snuck up on the trio as they ate grilled cheese sandwiches and discussed the case at the Main Street Diner.

"Geez, I didn't even realize it was dark outside. How long were we here?" asked Ava.

"At least a couple hours," said Carol, hurriedly throwing some money on the table.

Derik reached for his pocket, but Carol shook her head. "Don't worry about it; we gotta get going! You grab lunch next time."

"Wow," smiled Derik. "Thank you. You guys are awesome."

"We know," winked Ava playfully. "Now get going." She shoved Derik toward the door.

The girls stepped a few feet away from Derik, giving him some privacy while he called his dad.

"Okay," said Derik, looking a little less panicked. "He's still angry, but I managed to calm him down some."

"I'm sure he's got a lot on his mind right now," said Carol. "We'll walk with you to your house."

The trio took a shortcut through the center of town to save time. They hopped a fence at the Brown Recreation Center and trudged across the soccer field. The snow glistened and sparkled like tiny silver diamonds on a sea of felt beneath the moonlight.

"Everything looks so beautiful, so pristine," said Carol. "I almost hate to walk across the field, you know, it's completely untouched."

"Like your YouTube channel," snickered Ava.

"Har, har, so funny."

Derik stopped in his tracks. "Did you hear that?"

Ava pulled her earmuffs down from her ears. "What am I supposed to hear?"

"I hear it," said Carol. "It's a *buzzing*."

Suddenly a huge black drone screamed above them, flying only inches from their heads.

"Whoa," yelled Derik, ducking.

"What the—?! Run!" yelled Ava.

The children dove into the snow as the drone arched and dove again, rocketing through the air like a missile.

Carol sat up, looking around, trying to see who was controlling the drone.

"Crawl along the fence," yelled Derik, pointing to the fence that bordered the park. "It can't get us there!"

The trio scrambled toward the fence, fighting their way through the knee-high snow. Wham! The drone struck Carol in the back of the head, knocking her face down into the snow.

"Carol!" screamed Ava. She crawled through the snow to her. "Carol, are you okay?"

"I'm okay," said Carol, grabbing the back of her head, her vision filled with stars.

"It's about to dive again!" yelled Derik. "Come on! We gotta get to the fence."

Ava looked over her shoulder. She could see the drone make a tight circle in the sky. It raced toward them just as they reached the fence.

"Are you hurt, Carol?" asked Derik, concern filling his face.

"Just my pride," said Carol, gently shaking her head, still seeing stars.

The drone hung in the sky, buzzing like a giant mosquito, watching its prey.

"If we jump the fence and stay against it, the drone can't get us," said Ava.

"Great idea," said Derik.

The drone moved closer, hovering almost directly in front of them. A red light pulsed.

"It's recording us," whispered Carol.

Ava grabbed a handful of snow, packing it into a snowball. "Go away!" she yelled, hurling it at the drone. The drone remained motionless, unmoving, mocking her.

"I wish I had my baseball bat," said Derik angrily. "I'd go King Kong on that thing."

"Right now, we just need to get out of here," said Carol.

"Okay," agreed Derik. "On the count of three?"

Ava and Carol nodded.

"Ready...? One, two, three!" yelled Derik.

The trio spun and leapt up, grabbing the fence, pulling themselves up and over. They then fell to the ground on the other side in a tangled mass of arms and legs.

The drone rose high up in the sky, directly overhead, still watching.

"Okay," said Ava as they quickly untangled themselves. "We stick along the fence and then make a run for it between those houses. Then we stay close to the houses and trees until we get to Derik's house."

Derik and Carol nodded.

"All right," said Ava. "Let's go!"

But just as Ava's boot hit Fir Street, an angry roar erupted behind them.

"What?!" yelled Derik as a sleek black car came barreling toward them. They watched in horror as it launched off the street, rocketing up onto the sidewalk.

"Watch out!" screamed Carol, tackling Ava, knocking her out of the path of the car.

The car's engine revved as it slid off the sidewalk, just missing the children, fishtailing wildly as it hit the road.

"Derik, are you okay?" yelled Carol as she sat up.

"Yeah...," he whispered, barely able to speak.

They watched as the car slipped and slid around the corner, speeding away into the night.

"Obviously he failed driving school," said Ava, dropping her head back into the snow.

"They tried to kill us," Derik whispered.

Carol shook her head. *What did we get ourselves into?*

10
NEVER JUDGE A PICTURE BY A PICTURE

Carol stood in front of the crime board. It had been forty-eight hours since the first robbery, and so far, the only suspect was a sketch of a headless monster that Ava had affectionately named Brom Bones—the name of the headless horseman.

"This is driving me nuts. I can't tell what's what," said Carol, her nose literally pressed against the photo of the tunnel system.

"Well, we know this is the old church," said Ava, "and this is Main Street Diner…and this I think is Willerbees Antiques."

"That's weird," said Carol. "I thought that the tunnel system ran under the Hancock Museum…."

"It did," said Ava. "It's part of their tour. Remember, they have a glass enclosure around the entrance."

"Maybe that part of the tunnel was built after the photo?" proposed Carol.

"Or maybe it's a mistake," offered Ava. "We don't have anything to compare it to."

Carol's eyes lit up. "Oh, yes we do! Grab your coat; the museum closes in ten minutes!"

***

The girls stood at the top of the museum steps, their hands on their waists, their lungs heaving. Ava grabbed the door handle and pulled. It was locked. She smooshed her face against the glass. She could see light inside, but as far as she could tell there was no one inside.

"We're too late," said Carol, pointing to a small closed sign. "Everyone's closing early for the holidays."

"But they won't open again until after Christmas," groaned Ava. "It'll be too late."

The girls sat down on the steps, watching the endless stream of traffic. Every time they thought they were about to have a huge breakthrough in the case, something stopped them in their tracks.

"We're still no closer to solving this case than we were two days ago," said Carol.

"I know…we've been stumped before. I don't even know what to do next," said Ava.

"I would suggest getting out of the cold," said a singsong voice.

The girls' heads spun around. It was Gladys, the museum's concierge.

"Gladys!" yelled Ava. She jumped up, wrapping her arms around the petite, silver-haired woman.

"Hi, Gladys," beamed Carol, giving her a big hug.

"Come inside, come inside. You'll catch your death out here," she fussed, her brilliant gray-blue eyes sparkling just as brightly as ever.

Gladys worked the front desk at the museum. She had helped the girls solve the mysterious theft of the famous Ramesses diamonds and become a great friend.

"So," said Gladys, smiling, "what mischief are you two up to?"

"We're trying to solve another mystery," said Ava. "The bank and the jewelry store robberies."

"Oh, yes! I've been following that story in the news. Horrible, and right at the holidays."

"It is terrible," said Carol, nodding in agreement.

"How's your investigation going? Any spicy tidbits?"

"Well…it's kind of hit a roadblock," said Carol. "I thought for sure I was on to something. But, according to a map that we got from the public works building, I was wrong."

Gladys tilted her head. "How so?"

Carol turned back to Ava. "Can you grab the map out of my backpack and show Gladys?"

"Sure," smiled Ava. She pulled the map out, handing it to Carol.

"Why not spread it out on the desk, dear. That way I can see it a little more clearly."

"Good idea," agreed Carol, as she smoothed it out across the surface of the help desk. Gladys swiveled a desk lamp over the picture.

"See what I mean?" asked Carol, pointing to the map. "The tunnel system runs beneath the museum, but on this map it doesn't."

"Hmm....," Gladys studied the map intently. "Well, this isn't right...this isn't right at all. Where did you say you got this?"

"It's the official map from the public works building," said Carol.

Gladys looked at the map and then at Carol. "One second," said Gladys, holding up her finger. She fished around in her desk drawer for a moment and then pulled out a gargantuan magnifying glass. "Ah, perfect," said Gladys, holding it up to her eye.

"Whoa," whispered Ava. "Your eye is huge."

"Yes," laughed Gladys. "Wait until you're eighty; there are all kinds of little surprises. Okay," continued Gladys, leaning in. "Yes, the signature beneath the seal...it says Wilbur Jones."

"Is that bad?" asked Ava.

"Not bad; it's just that Wilbur Jones died in 1842, and the map is dated 1846."

The Haunted Mansion

"Who was Wilbur Jones?" asked Carol.

"He was the head of the town council. His signature is on many of the maps and prints here."

"That's why we're here...not because of the signature, but we want to compare this map with the one upstairs."

"Let's do it," replied Gladys excitedly. She snatched the photo off the desk and began walking briskly toward the stairs. "Well...don't just stand there like a couple of statues," she said over her shoulder. "Come on!"

The girls followed Gladys up the winding staircase and down the hall to the History of Livingston exhibit. Gladys flicked on the lights. The walls were filled with fascinating black-and-white photos displaying an illustrative timeline of the history of Livingston. It was fascinating to see historical landmarks that were built two hundred years ago still being used today.

However, Carol only had one thing in mind, and that was the massive photo of Livingston taken in the 1860s by an aerial blimp. And that picture just happened to hang at the very back of the exhibit. Beneath it was an amazing illustration of the intricate tunnel system that serpentined beneath the town.

Carol's heart began to race. She had already spotted it. It was as clear as day. The tunnel system ran directly beneath the bank and the jewelry store!

"Look, Ava!" Carol cried out. "The tunnel, it passes directly beneath the bank—"

"And the jewelry store," said Ava excitedly.

Gladys stretched out the map Carol had brought her beneath the picture. The tunnel systems were remarkably different from each other.

"Who gave you this map?" asked Gladys.

"A man who works at the public works building. Hector…Harold…"

"Harvey," interrupted Ava. "Harvey Cooper."

"That's right," nodded Carol.

"Hmm," frowned Gladys. "I don't know anyone named Harvey, but I do know for certain that this is not the original document. It's a fake."

"So, Harvey duped us?" asked Carol angrily.

"Someone did," nodded Gladys. "Not necessarily Harvey. He may have been fooled as well."

"I don't know," said Ava. "He seemed to know a lot about the map, remember? He knew the location of every landmark."

"Why would he go to the trouble of creating a fake map?" mused Carol.

"I think you know the answer to that," said Gladys.

"Gladys," said Carol, pointing to the photo, "this narrow road is Mall Street, but I don't see Whitmore Street."

"This is Whitmore Street, right here," replied Gladys, tapping the map, "and this is the location of the old Butcher house."

"But…it says morgue," said Carol, confused.

"Well, actually, it was a hospital and a morgue. During the Revolutionary War, Samuel Butcher used the top floor as a makeshift hospital, the first floor to perform his surgeries, and the bottom floor as a morgue."

"Eeesh, no wonder there are so many scary stories about that house," said Ava.

"What's scary is Mr. Butcher never had any type of medical training. Ironically, Samuel Butcher was actually—"

"A butcher," said Carol, finishing her sentence.

"That's right," agreed Gladys. "The stories that I have read would give you nightmares. Many said that Samuel lived up to his last name."

She paused, letting this sink in.

"When Samuel died, his children renovated the house and tried to put the past behind them, but many people in the town, well…they never forgot about Samuel's atrocities. So, a long time ago, in the middle of the night, the Butchers simply disappeared, leaving everything behind."

"That is officially creepy…and sad," whispered Ava.

"Yes, yes, it is," agreed Gladys.

"Carol…I'm gonna need that night-light back," said Ava.

"Gladys," said Carol, staring at the tunnel system, "it looks like the tunnel system extended all the way out to the Butcher house."

"Yes, it did. Actually, it was one of the first sections of the tunnel built in 1775. If you follow it with your finger, you can see that it leads to the old church. Many of the graves that you see behind that church are filled with patients from the Butcher house."

"Last question, I promise," said Carol. "It looks like there's a small section of tunnel that leads from the Butcher house to Crispin Pond?"

"Ah, yes, Crispin Pond. That was a small, man-made reservoir. At one time a huge portion of the Livingston community used it for water. They drained it about fifty years ago. It's conservation land now."

Carol remained silent for a moment, chewing on her bottom lip. "Gladys, I think you may have just blown this case wide open."

Gladys's eyes sparkled, and her face filled with pride. "Us girls gotta do what we gotta do to keep this town safe," she said, laughing.

Carol gave her a conspiratorial smile. "Yes, ma'am, we do."

Gladys led the girls downstairs and back into the lobby.

"Thank you so much," said Carol, giving Gladys a big hug. "We promise to keep you in the loop!"

"You better!" smiled Gladys. "You better!"

The Haunted Mansion

It was 8 p.m. when they stepped out of the museum. In the distance, the deep tones of the church bell filled the night.

"Eight o'clock," said Carol, breaking into a run. "Come on!"

II
TUNNEL VISION

Ava and Carol lay flat on their bellies, staring across a shallow, snow-covered ravine, which they had learned from Gladys, used to be Crispin Pond. Now, it resembled a moon crater filled with rocks and scraggly bushes poking through the snow. There was, however, one other thing that brought a smile to Carol's lips: tire tracks. And those tracks disappeared behind a wall of dirt and rocks.

It was pitch-black outside, except for the occasional break in the clouds, revealing a full moon.

"Can your blood freeze?" whispered Ava through chattering teeth.

"Only your brain can freeze; so, in your case, you have nothing to worry about."

"If you're implying that I—"

"Shhh, voices!" whispered Carol excitedly.

Ava nodded. She could hear the voices—and their feet crunching across the snow. Seconds later, car doors slammed shut.

"They're leaving," whispered Carol.

The car engine struggled. Ava could imagine the man turning the key and pressing the gas pedal over and over. Finally, the engine roared to life. Thick smoke billowed upward from behind the rock wall.

"Thank goodness," whispered Ava. "For a moment I thought we were gonna have to push them."

Moments later, the car appeared. It was the perfect car if you wanted to go unnoticed: an older model, dark gray Toyota. The car stopped for a moment as the driver rolled down his window, took one more hard drag of his cigarette, and then flicked it away in a fiery arch. The girls were close enough to hear it sizzle as it hit the snow.

The car slowly crept away as the driver closed his window, snow crunching under its tires. It seemed to take an eternity for the car to cross the ravine and pull onto the main road. Ava and Carol didn't move until the red taillights had completely disappeared into the darkness.

"Okay," said Carol, slowly standing. "Let's go."

"Wait," said Ava, grabbing Carol's arm. "We can't just walk across the ravine; they'll see our footprints."

"What do you suggest—we fly?"

"Yes. I have a pouch of this glittery powder; just sprinkle some on top of your head…."

"Ava! Seriously."

"Fine, follow me," said Ava. "I saw this in a movie."

Ava worked her way down the rocky incline until she reached the edge of the ravine. She then sprawled belly-down onto the snow.

"Well?" she asked, looking over her shoulder.

"I'm coming, I'm coming," said Carol.

Carol joined Ava, and like two water spiders they traveled across the snow to where the car had appeared. There was a massive hill made of dirt and rock that the thieves had used as a natural barrier to hide their car behind.

Unsure what lay on the other side, Carol crept along the bottom of the hill. She grabbed her phone and clicked on the photo app. Slowly she extended her arm, using her phone to see what was around the corner.

"Whoa," whispered Carol.

"What is it?" asked Ava.

"Come here—you've got to see this."

Ava scooched over beside Carol as she adjusted the phone so Ava could see the screen. Just beyond the wall was a huge slab of cement resembling a giant pizza oven, the opening sealed by an enormous iron plate that looked like a manhole cover—only the cover had a gaping two-foot hole cut through the center of it.

Ava let out a low whistle; the entrance to the tunnel was pitch-black. "I hope you're not claustrophobic...."

Carol held up her phone and took a couple pictures. "Just in case," she smiled unconvincingly.

Ava grabbed her Thor 2000 flashlight from her backpack and flicked it on. "All right," she said, shining it into the entrance of the cave. "It's now or never."

The first thing the girls noticed once inside was the dank, earthy smell that permeated the tunnel.

"Ugh," moaned Ava. "It stinks in here."

"Try breathing through your mouth," offered Carol.

Ava played the beam of her flashlight along the ceiling and walls. Jagged chunks of rock and roots erupted from the sides and top of the tunnel. The floor was made of packed earth, and the ceiling was supported by thick beams of wood that looked like railroad ties. The only source of light came from Ava's flashlight, which was powerful enough to let them see well into the distance.

"It must have taken forever to dig this tunnel," said Ava. "And it's still in amazing condition."

"It is," agreed Carol, checking her phone. "They've been gone seven minutes. We gotta move fast. If we get caught, we're goners."

"Okay," said Ava, picking up her pace. "No need to—"

Ava stopped in her tracks. She put her hand on Carol's shoulder as she flicked off the flashlight. The darkness of the cave was suffocating. Carol fought the panic rising up through her body. *Breathe,* Carol told herself. *Breathe.*

"Do you see it?" whispered Ava.

Carol nodded. She could see it. The faintest of light shone up ahead. Using their hands on the walls of the tunnel, they moved forward until they reached the source of the light.

There was a wooden ladder that led to what looked like a trap door. Light in the yellowish-orange range escaped around the edges, and a looped string hung down close to the ladder.

"It's like the access door to my attic," whispered Carol. "You pull the string and it opens."

"Got it," whispered Ava.

"Only problem is we don't know if there's anyone inside."

"I got that covered," whispered Ava. She grabbed her phone and reached in her backpack.

"A selfie stick?" asked Carol.

"Watch and learn." Ava attached her phone to the selfie stick and then opened the FaceTime app. Carol's phone buzzed.

"It's me—answer it," Ava said helpfully.

"Ahh," Carol's face lit up. "I see what you're doing."

"You catch on fast," smiled Ava. "Wish me luck!"

Ava placed a foot on the first rung of the ladder; it felt sturdy. She climbed up to the top of the ladder, and with one hand pulled ever so gently on the string. The access door opened just a smidge, bathing Ava's face in light and making her grimace.

Carefully, she raised her phone through the opening, and then, using her selfie stick, she slowly rotated her phone 360 degrees.

Using FaceTime, Carol was able to see everything in the room. "Ava," she called up in a low voice. "The room's empty!"

"Here goes nothing!" Ava pulled on the string, completely opening the access door. Warm air and light filled the tunnel. Ava paused at the top of the ladder, letting her eyes adjust to the light. Then, she slowly pulled herself up through the opening into the room.

Ava spun around, doing a quick surveil. The room officially gave her the creeps. She crouched over the opening and gave Carol the thumbs-up. Ava trembled as Carol climbed the ladder; she was sure someone was going to sneak up behind her.

She breathed a sigh of relief as Carol's head popped through the opening. Ava grabbed her by the forearm and pulled her onto the floor.

"Holy moly," said Carol, looking around. "This place is disgusting."

Ava nodded her head as she slowly lowered the trap door.

"See what you can find, and fast!" directed Ava.

The room was lit by a single lightbulb and a tall, skinny lamp held together by duct tape. Two makeshift desks made from cardboard boxes sat in the center of the room. Each desk had a laptop and was connected to wireless hotspots. In front of the desk was a standing children's chalkboard, filled with images and maps.

The windows were covered with thick black cardboard. In the far corner of the room, black coveralls hung on a makeshift clothes rack constructed of wooden dowels suspended from the ceiling by fishing wire. Beneath the coveralls were three large backpacks and a machine on wheels that looked like some kind of generator.

Ava pulled at the corner of one of the pieces of cardboard covering the window. She crouched down and squinted through the opening. It took a moment to get her bearings, and then she realized exactly where they were.

"You were right, Carol. We're in the Butcher house. It's the basement."

Carol nodded. She was staring at the chalkboard, her hands on her hips. "Ava, come here quick! Look at this!"

Ava rushed over to Carol's side. "Here's the map of the tunnel system. Look right here," she said, jabbing excitedly. A red circle was drawn around the bank and the jewelry store.

"Carol…there's a—"

"I know," said Carol. She stared at the third circle; it was drawn around Archie's Collectibles.

"Why Archie's Collectibles? Are they gonna get matching lockets?"

"No. Remember, these guys seem to like things quick and easy. My guess is they're after his collection of rare baseball cards. Remember his pride and joy, the Babe Ruth card? That card alone is worth seven hundred thousand dollars."

"Oh yeah," said Ava, "and he has some super valuable comics...."

"Ava, take some pics of the board. I'm gonna see what else I can find, and I'm setting my alarm for five minutes."

"Good idea," agreed Ava as she grabbed her camera and began taking pictures.

While Ava grabbed evidence, Carol began rummaging through the papers on top of the makeshift desks. Not expecting anything to happen, she tapped on the track pad. The laptop jumped to life, displaying a web page that said their travel itinerary had been emailed to them. Carol's heart began pounding...there was a Gmail tab open in the browser. "Please! Please," she whispered. She clicked the tab, and there it was: an email from JetBlue.

"Yes! Um, Ava," began Carol, "I'm pretty sure they are going to rob Archie's Collectibles tonight."

"Tonight, as in *tonight*?"

"They have a 5:20 a.m. flight out of Rhode Island, and get this: They're going to Mexico City."

"If they get to Mexico," worried Ava, "they'll disappear forever."

"That's why we have to stop them," said Carol, scribbling the flight information on a scrap of paper.

"If we can find where they hid the diamonds and money, they can't leave! They won't leave without that," said Ava.

Carol glanced worriedly at her phone; they had three minutes to find the stolen goods and get out of the house.

"Where do you think they would have hidden it?" asked Ava as she flew around the room, searching under tarps, boxes, and mountains of junk. "There's, like, a million hiding places."

"Could be anywhere," said Carol. "They have this entire house. It could be in the walls, under a loose floorboard.... It could...."

Carol paused; her heart began to beat wildly. She could hear voices coming from the tunnel!

"Ava! Ava! They're coming."

12
A DARING ESCAPE

Ava spun in a circle. "The stairs!" she whispered urgently, pointing to a narrow stairwell that ran against the back wall. The girls raced over to the stairs, cringing as the old staircase creaked and groaned under their weight.

An old wooden door was all that stood in their way of escape! Ava grabbed the doorknob and twisted. It was locked. *Maybe it's just stuck,* she hoped. Ava grasped the handle with both hands and twisted. The doorknob didn't budge!

Ava turned to Carol wild-eyed, her heart pounding. They could hear the sound of footsteps climbing the ladder.

"Hide!" hissed Ava. "Hide!"

The girls stormed down the steps, just as the access door began to rise.

"Back here," whispered Carol. Ava followed Carol through a dark doorway into a small laundry room.

Ava scrambled onto an old washing machine and tore the black cardboard from the window.

"What are you doing?" asked Carol, panicking.

"Escaping. Watch the door!"

Carol crouched in the doorway, staring at the trap door. A gloved hand appeared and then a man's face—short blond hair, jagged bangs, square jaw. Carol shrank back into the shadows.

"Come on, stupid window," growled Ava through clenched teeth.

"Ava, hurry!"

Ava tugged on the window frame with all her might. Suddenly, giant cracks raced across the thin, narrow pane. Shards of glass fell from the window into the snow, leaving a row of jagged pieces, like razor-sharp fangs along the bottom of the frame. *That works,* she thought.

"Almost got it. Just need to pull these pieces out," said Ava, desperation filling her voice.

"It's too late! Get down," pleaded Carol. "They're here!"

"I've almost got it," whispered Ava. "Stall them!"

"How?" asked Carol incredulously.

Carol quickly took in her surroundings. *Washing machine, dryer, metal shelves, hot water heater, and a nasty sink with gross brown stains.* Carol shook her head. This wasn't good. They were trapped!

Cold sweat ran down Ava's neck. Her hands were trembling so badly that she cut herself repeatedly on the razor-sharp glass. It didn't help that less than twenty feet away she could hear the thieves' voices. She could make out a woman's voice and two men.

They must be eating, she thought, as the smell of Chinese food filled the air. She dared to steal a quick glance over her shoulder.

Carol was lying on the floor, her phone out. She was using it to spy on the bad guys. Ava looked back at the window. It wasn't perfect, but she had removed enough glass for them to make it through. She placed the cardboard back over the window, hiding the missing glass.

Soundlessly, Ava lowered herself from the washing machine onto the cement floor and crawled over to Carol.

"It's ready," whispered Ava.

"Okay," replied Carol softly. "They're eating. It's now or never."

The girls crawled over to the washing machine. They stopped and listened. The conversation had turned to their Archie's Collectibles heist.

Ava climbed up on top of the washing machine. She removed the black cardboard, placing it outside the window, and then carefully pulled herself through the basement window and out into the snow.

Crouching beside the window, Ava turned to help Carol through.

"Careful," Ava whispered, "there's a lot of glass." Ava waited...no response. "Carol?" Ava whispered.

Something must have gone wrong! What if they come in the room and see the cardboard missing and the broken window? Ava grabbed the cardboard and placed it over the window. She shook her head; it felt like she was trapping Carol in the room. *What do I do?*

Carol had just climbed up onto the washing machine when she heard a chair scrape across the floor. Someone was up and moving!

She tried to let Ava know what was happening, but it was too late—footsteps were moving toward the laundry room.

Dropping to the floor, she squeezed between the wall and the washing machine.

A dim overhead bulb flicked on. Glowing spots danced in Carol's eyes as they adjusted to the light. Each footstep sounded like thunder as it came closer to where she was hidden. She willed her body to stop shaking. The footsteps stopped. From around the washer, she could see a huge boot and leg—and then a horrific screeching sound. This was it; it was all over!

Carol mentally kicked herself, *get a grip*, the screeching sound was merely the dryer door being opened. Air rushed out of Carol's lungs like a slowly deflating tire. He was doing laundry. Carol could hear the man breathing as he moved the clothes from the washing machine into the dryer. The man slammed the dryer door shut, and with a press of a button, the dryer whirred to life.

"Please. Please. Please," prayed Carol. "Please leave."

Seconds later, her prayers were answered. The light flicked off, and once again she was bathed in darkness. Slowly, Carol crawled to the doorway. The man from the laundry room had joined a tall man with a blond crew cut and a petite but athletic-looking woman at the chalkboard.

The sound from the dryer was a two-edged sword. It would cover any noise that Carol made, but it also made it almost impossible to hear the bad guys. Carol made a quick calculation in her head. From the chalkboard to the utility room…at least two or three seconds. That was all she needed.

Ava was going crazy. Carol was trapped and she had to get her out. Somehow, she needed to draw the thieves' attention away from the laundry room. *The front door!* Yes, she would bang on the front door, and then….

Ava jumped backward as Carol burst through the window, pushing the cardboard away with her head.

"Carol! Carol!" screamed Ava, grabbing her by the arms and pulling her through the window. "You're okay! That was too close."

"It was nothing," said Carol, replacing the cardboard over the window. She looked at Ava and smiled. "Come on, it's time to take these guys down!"

13
POLICE PAJAMAS...IT'S A THING

Derik was listening to music when he felt his phone vibrate. The text appeared on his screen: *Backyard, hurry!* He ran to his bedroom window and looked out. Below, Ava and Carol were waving frantically.

He threw his headphones on his bed and rushed downstairs. His dad's Christmas party was in full swing. He grabbed a jacket from a hook as he sprinted down the hallway and out the back door.

"Ava! Carol!" he yelled. "What's going on?"

"We found the bad guys," said Ava, her voice filled with excitement.

"You did?! Where?"

"We'll explain everything to you, but right now we really need your help," replied Carol.

"Okay," nodded Derik. "How can I help?"

"Is Archie...?" Carol paused. "I don't even know Archie's last name. The guy that owns Archie's Collectibles, is he here?"

"Yes, his whole family is here…it's a virtual 'who's who' of Livingston inside."

"What about Detective Edwards?" asked Ava.

Derik thought for a moment. "I think so. I know Lieutenant Norris is here."

"I don't know Lieutenant Norris well enough," said Carol.

"Okay, I'll check. If he is, what do I say?"

"We need you to discreetly let Detective Edwards know that we're outside, and we need to talk to him. *Discreet,* being the keyword."

"He's a family friend," said Ava. "He won't ask any questions, just tell him we need his help."

"Got it," said Derik, turning toward the door.

"Wait," called out Carol. "One thing…right now, we don't know who's helping the thieves. We have to be careful—we don't want to tip them off."

"I understand," he said, holding up his hands. "Don't worry," Derik smiled. "I'll just yell for him from across the room the moment I see him."

"Perfect," smiled Ava. "You should turn off the lights when you yell his name. The more pandemonium, the better."

"Got it, discreet pandemonium. I'll be back in a flash," said Derik as he disappeared inside.

He wasn't kidding. Seconds later, Derik appeared, followed by Detective Edwards. As always, the detective was dressed in an impeccably tailored three-piece suit, his hair perfectly combed above eyebrows that accentuated his dark-brown, brooding eyes. A single hand-stitched snowflake adorned his festive, ruby-red silk tie.

Ava imagined that he probably had official police pajamas that he slept in, just in case someone broke the law in his dreams.

"Ava, Carol, everything okay? What's going on?" he asked, a concerned look on his face.

"We're fine, Mr. Edwards. We just needed to talk to you in private," said Ava.

"Okay," he said, clasping his hands. "What's this all about?"

"There's going to be a robbery tonight," started Carol.

"Carol, how do you know…?"

"I'm sorry," said Ava, interrupting him. "We can't really talk here," said Ava eyeing the door.

"We know that there is at least one person on the inside who helped orchestrate the robberies here in Livingston. They may even be here at the party," clarified Carol.

"All right," said Detective Edwards. "I'll get my car. We can go to the police station."

Ava and Carol looked at each other and shook their heads. "So far, the bad guys have been one step ahead of us, and if they see us going to the police station, it might spook them," said Ava.

"We have to proceed carefully; we know that we are being watched," said Carol.

"It's true," nodded Ava, "One of the bad guys tried to decapitate her with a drone. And…they may have at one time…tried to run over us with a car."

"Run over you with a car?! What?!" Detective Edwards exclaimed. "Ava, why didn't you report this?"

"I'm telling you now—it happened this evening. If I had said anything earlier, the bad guys would have gotten away. Plus my parents would have barricaded me in my room until I was thirty-nine. My parents said I could get married when I was thirty-nine," said Ava noticing Derik's strange expression. "Please, Blake—I mean, Mr. Edwards—Carol has a plan to catch these guys. We just need your help."

Detective Edwards's face grew taut as he exhaled sharply. "Fine! But from now on, no more secrets, understood?!"

"Yes, sir," the trio chorused, doing their best to look remorseful.

"Okay," said Detective Edwards, "where do you suggest we plan our attack, since the police station doesn't seem to be an option?"

Ava and Carol turned to each other, already knowing the answer—"The Lair," answered Ava, smiling. "The Lair."

14
CAROL'S PLAN

The night burst into a flurry of activity. From the safety of The Lair, Carol took Detective Edwards step-by-step through her plan for catching the crooks. Ava could tell from the look on his face that he was amazed at how Carol had connected all of the individual pieces of evidence on the crime board.

While Carol worked her magic, Ava called Gladys, asking for her help. She gave the group a thumbs-up as she hung up the phone.

"She'll meet us at the museum and have everything ready," announced Ava.

Derik was busy on the phone as well, grabbing the last piece of the puzzle that would complete the operation. "I promise, I promise." He nodded his head as he talked. "Yes, sir. Thank you so much."

"We got it," Derik smiled. "Mr. Roberts will drop off the cleaning van at Green Central Parking Deck in thirty minutes."

"Perfect," said Carol, nodding. "My dad is on the way over with his car. Detective Edwards is going to drive us to the parking deck, where we'll meet Lieutenant Norris and his men."

"So, we're all hiding in the cleaning van?" asked Ava.

"Yep, we'll all hide in the van, which will take us to the delivery zone behind the museum. There's a massive canopy over the delivery area. We'll be able to sneak into the museum without being seen," said Carol.

"I must tell you, I'm extremely impressed," said Detective Edwards, smiling. "I may have to replace my team with you guys."

"Don't you guys have to do tons of paperwork?" asked Ava.

"Oh, yeah," nodded Detective Edwards, "we have reports for everything, even reports for reports."

Ava looked over at Carol, whose eyes were glassing over. "*Reports*," Carol whispered dreamily.

"Carol! Snap out of it. Sorry, Blake—I mean, Detective Edwards—we're more like 'bull in a china shop' types of detectives. We wreak mayhem, break a few things, and then quietly walk away."

"So close," sighed Carol, shaking her head at Ava. "So close."

"Oh," added Ava. "I forgot to mention, we always get the bad guy."

"Or girl," added Derik.

"Or girl," smiled Ava. "We have a certain image to uphold."

"Okay," said Detective Edwards, glancing at his watch. "That was a little more than I expected.... Let's get this show on the road."

"This is going to be epic," smiled Ava. "Absolutely epic!"

15
WORTHINGTON TUNNEL EXHIBIT

10:17 P.M. Worthington Tunnel, Hancock Museum

Ava, Carol, Derik—and what appeared to be Livingston's entire police force—stood at the entrance to the Worthington Tunnel Exhibit. A four-inch-thick glass enclosure surrounded the opening to the tunnel. A podium in front of the display contained a detailed map of the tunnel system.

Gladys motioned everyone over to the podium. "This red dot designates the Worthington Tunnel entrance." She traced her finger along the map, "You'll need to follow this passage until you reach the main tunnel."

"Are there any markings? Anything to navigate by?" asked Detective Edwards.

"No need," said Gladys. "This passage will take you to the main tunnel. You'll make a left...," Gladys moved her finger up the map, "...for about...," she paused while she counted the little lines on the map that designated twenty-foot sections, "…about six hundred feet."

"Anyone have a six-hundred-foot ruler?" laughed one of the police officers.

"You don't need one," answered Carol. "The average adult walking step is about 2.1 feet. So, once we reach the main tunnel, it will be about…," she paused, doing the math in her head.

"Two hundred and eighty-five steps," smiled Derik.

"Ohhhhh, you stole Carol's thunder," winked Ava.

"What? My dad's a banker," laughed Derik. "Numbers are in my DNA."

"*Your* number's gonna be up, if you mess with her *moment* again," said Ava, making air quotes.

"So," said Detective Edwards, "we follow the first passage, make a left at the main tunnel, walk 285 steps, and we should be there."

"Exactly," nodded Gladys. "There is a small passage that leads directly under Archie's Collectibles."

"Perfect," smiled Detective Edwards.

"Sir, I have a question," said Officer McCoy, looking pale and worried. "Why are we taking the tunnel? I mean, couldn't we just use the cleaning van?" he shrugged.

Ava looked at the police officer. A thin line of sweat glistened across his forehead, just under his spikey blond buzz cut. *Someone is not a fan of dark and confining spaces*, thought Ava.

"Two reasons. First, we know that they are surveilling their targets via a drone. If they see anything suspicious, they're gonna cut their losses and vanish. Secondly, they're not going to break into a building that is occupied," said Detective Edwards.

"Okay," nodded Officer McCoy, sounding defeated.

"Our biggest hurdle is going to be the grate that is used for drainage in his restoration room. Archie said that there's a massive lock on it, and as far as he knows, it hasn't been opened in over fifty years. We'll have to cut through the lock, breach the grate, replace the lock, and get into position before the suspects arrive."

"Won't they be suspicious if they see a new lock?" asked Officer Louis.

"No, thanks to Gladys," replied Detective Edwards. "She has given us a beautiful lock from the 1950s. Unfortunately," he said, turning to Gladys, "they are probably going to melt it into a pile of glob."

"It's a small sacrifice for the greater good," smiled Gladys.

Derik nudged Ava. "Someone's an Avengers fan."

"Once we're in position," continued Detective Edwards, "we'll wait for the suspects to enter Archie's. Once they're inside, I'll send an alert to Lieutenant Norris and Officer Louis. They'll position themselves below the grate in case the suspects attempt to escape back into the tunnel."

"What about the drone operator?" asked Officer Davis. Ava and Carol both recognized Officer Davis from the bank. She was short, compact, and athletic, with a fiery stare that could melt ice.

"Officer Tiny and Wilks will be stationed half a mile away in separate cruisers. Once the suspects are in the store, we'll alert them to move in. The drone operator should be close by. Any more questions?" asked Detective Edwards, eyeing the group. "Good. Get your gear on, check your radios, and we'll get moving." He turned his attention to Ava and Carol.

"We know," said Ava. "We hide in the reading room until either you, or another officer, comes to get us."

"Exactly," he smiled. "No exceptions."

"Yes, sir," said the trio, nodding in unison.

"All right," barked Detective Edwards as he stepped into the tunnel's entrance. "Let's do this."

Gladys punched a code into the alarm box connected to the enclosure and then unlocked the heavy glass door. She gave Ava and Carol a big hug.

"Be safe," she whispered, her voice filled with worry as they disappeared into the tunnel.

16
TOO CLOSE FOR COMFORT

The narrow tunnel was dark and musty. Giant spiderwebs stretched across the group's path, covering them in sticky goo. Spiders' eyes glistened creepily in the light from their headlamps. The air was cool, but it felt thick and smothering, like being wrapped in a wet blanket.

Up ahead, Ava couldn't help but feel sorry for Officer McCoy. His breathing was erratic, and his nose sounded like a cheap whistle. She grabbed the collapsible ladder he was carrying, hoping that would at least help a little.

Up ahead, she could see Detective Edwards swatting down spiderwebs. *Where do all of the spiders go when he knocks down their webs? Never mind.* She shivered at the thought of it. *I don't want to know.*

Suddenly, the passage opened up into a massive tunnel. A network of large wooden support beams arched upward and spanned across the top of the tunnel, reinforcing the ceiling.

"Amazing," whispered Carol, surprised that the beams looked to be in surprisingly good shape over a century later. She wished she could take a picture for her father, an architect—maybe later.

"Okay, this is the main section of the tunnel," said Detective Edwards, shifting his backpack. "Which means," he continued, "we're about three minutes from Archie's. Keep your eyes and ears open."

"I like this much better," whispered Ava, "way less spiderwebs."

Carol nodded. "It's crazy that this huge tunnel runs below our town and hardly anyone knows about it."

"You could literally drive a car through here," added Derik. "Insane!"

"I hope I'm right about this…. What if the bad guys decide to go somewhere else, or they just disappear? What if the plans we saw were just a decoy?" Carol whispered worriedly.

"Carol, you're overthinking things," said Ava, switching the ladder to her other hand. "They have no idea that *anyone* saw their plans. These guys think they are invincible, and that, my friend, is what's gonna be their downfall!"

"I guess so," whispered Carol.

"I know so," smiled Ava.

Detective Edwards signaled for everyone to stop as he slipped into a narrow passageway. Moments later he reappeared. "This is it!" he whispered excitedly.

Officer Davis took up guard position at the entrance while the rest of the team moved single file into the tunnel. The passage opened up into a rectangular room about the size of a small shed. Officer McCoy placed a flashlight vertically against the dirt wall, illuminating the room.

The room had large wooden support beams with huge metal girders that supported a concrete foundation. In the center of the ceiling was a huge metal grate, with a massive padlock that looked to be a hundred years old.

Detective Edwards shrugged off his backpack and removed a crowbar and pair of bolt cutters. Ava opened the ladder directly below the grate.

Carol opened the flashlight app on her phone and aimed the light at the padlock.

"Thanks, Carol," said Detective Edwards as he scrambled up the ladder. He carefully guided the bolt cutters through the shackle of the lock and squeezed with all his might. He twisted and twisted in a sawing motion—Carol winced at the amount of noise he was making.

After struggling for a couple minutes, he jumped to the ground and turned to Officer McCoy. "I can't make a dent in this thing—you try."

No matter how much McCoy grunted, twisted, and squeezed, the lock wouldn't budge. He climbed down the ladder, his face red from exertion and frustration.

"We should have brought Tiny," he said, wiping the sweat from his hands. "He probably could have broken the lock with his bare hands."

Tiny wouldn't have fit through the first tunnel. Detective Edwards grabbed the bolt cutters and attacked the lock again, twisting and pulling. Sweat poured down his face into his eyes. He stared up at the grate, shaking his head.

"Sir," said Carol, "I have an—"

Officer Davis raced into the room. "I can hear voices! They're coming."

Ava thought Detective Edwards's teeth were going to shatter before the lock. He slammed the handles of the bolt lock together, cutting into the shackle of the lock, making small cuts into the metal, but unable to cut all the way through.

"I have an idea," said Carol more forcefully.

"What?" said Detective Edwards hotly. "I'm—I'm sorry, Carol. What is it?"

"I've seen my dad's workmen do this on the job site. Officer Davis needs to push the crowbar through the shackles—she'll twist while you cut. Since there's only one ladder...," she turned to Officer McCoy, "...she's gonna need to stand on your back."

Carol had barely gotten the words out of her mouth before Officer McCoy was on the ground on his hands and knees and Officer Davis was standing on his back. Carol handed her the crowbar and grabbed her around the hips to hold her steady while Ava grabbed the ladder.

"I'm going to see where they are," said Derik, racing out of the room. Derik's heart beat wildly in his chest. As soon as he stepped into the main tunnel, he could hear voices moving toward him. Voices—and a loud, repetitive squeaking noise. *The plasma cutter,* he thought. *That's what's making the squeaking noise.*

Detective Edwards opened the bolt cutter wide and twisted it into place. "On the count of three," he said. "One! Two! Three!" A loud grating sound filled the room as dirt and debris rained down on top of them. Ava and Carol cringed at the noise.

"What is up with this lock?!" asked Detective Edwards incredulously, wiping the dirt from his face.

The voices were much closer now! Derik could see flickers of light flashing on the walls of the tunnel. He raced into the room. "They're almost here," he said urgently. "I can see their flashlights!"

Detective Edwards nodded at Officer Davis. "Give it everything you got! On the count of three. One! Two! Three!" Carol could see the tendons in Officer Davis's neck as she twisted with all her might.

There was a loud scraping sound of metal on metal, and then—*POW!* It sounded like a gunshot as the shackle snapped in two. It took a moment for Detective Edwards to realize what had happened before he started urgently whispering, "Move! Move!" He pushed up on the heavy grate and slid it aside.

Ava rushed out and grabbed Derik. She could hear the voices clearly. They had maybe forty-five seconds at best!

"Carol, you first," said Detective Edwards. "Remember, straight to the reading room and hide."

"Yes, sir," she whispered as he lifted her up and helped her through the grate. He helped Officer Davis up next and then quickly handed her the backpack and ladder. "Ava, Derik, you're next!"

He quickly helped everyone else through the grate. The squeaking of the wheels stopped; he could hear a male voice say, "This is it." They were at the entrance! He leapt up, grasping the edge of the grate. And with the help of Officers Davis and McCoy, the detective was pulled into the room. Without a second of hesitation, they quietly slid the grate back into place.

Detective Edwards had just enough time to replace the lock with the decoy when one of the thieves shone their flashlight directly at the grate. Suddenly, a whooshing sound filled the room, followed by a bright blue flame that began melting the lock away.

Detective Edwards and his team disappeared into the darkness. They had made it, and not a second too soon.

17
ARCHIE'S COLLECTIBLES

Ava, Carol, and Derik scampered behind a cream-colored sofa closest to the front door. Ava peeked over the couch, scanning the reading room. There was a fireplace, two more cream-colored couches, and a half-dozen chairs with long, flat tables in front of them. A variety of potted plants were placed in each corner, and the walls were filled with colorful covers of super-old comic books.

Ava dropped back beside Derik and Carol. "I hate being stuck in the reading room…it's like being banished to a library."

"A library with cool furniture," added Derik.

"Shhh!" whispered Carol, placing a finger to her lips.

The trio listened intently; they could hear the plasma torch fire up, the grate being moved to the side, and then footsteps. Heavy footsteps.

"Here they come," whispered Carol excitedly.

***

Detective Edwards's fingers swiped across his phone, sending out a text he had already prepared: *Deploy*.

He knew that as soon as Lieutenant Norris got the message, his team would be on the way. He held up four fingers to Officers

McCoy and Davis. The thieves would get the surprise of their lives in four minutes.

The thieves were professionals; they worked quickly and efficiently. A tall man in a black hoodie rolled what looked like a cooler on wheels across the floor and down the hallway. He paused at a large wooden door and nodded to a shaggy red-haired man in a green hoodie. The man jammed a crowbar into the doorframe and yanked. The wood cracked and splintered around the lock.

"Good enough," said the man in the black hoodie. He took a step back and kicked the door open.

"Like taking candy from a baby," he laughed evilly.

"A rich baby," replied the other thief.

Seconds later, a familiar whooshing sound filled the office.

***

"He must have his safe hidden in his office," whispered Derik bitterly.

The girls nodded. Anger surged through Carol's veins. They had destroyed his door, and now they were destroying his safe. *What is taking Detective Edwards so long?*

Detective Edwards looked at his watch and took in a deep breath. In sixty seconds, Lieutenant Norris would be in position. Suddenly, a woman with a shaved head and black combat boots was standing less than five feet from where he was hiding.

He watched as she crouched below a series of glass display cases. *What is she doing?* She flicked a switch, and a little green light went out. *She is turning off the alarms!* The woman removed a pair of bolt cutters from her jacket and began cutting off the locks.

Detective Edwards signaled to his team: It was *go time*.

"Livingston Police!" yelled Officer Davis, rushing toward the thief with the shaved head. The woman whipped around. If she was surprised, it didn't show. She raised her hands in the air, a smirk on her face.

"Well, hello, Officer," she smiled.

"Drop the bolt cutters, now!" said Officer Davis, drawing her taser, inching closer toward her.

"Oh, these?" said the woman coyly.

"Drop them now! I won't ask—"

Officer Davis dove to the side as the bolt cutters whipped past her head, sinking into the wall with a deep thud. She covered her head with her arms as a heavy lamp came crashing down onto her.

The woman hurdled over the display case and raced through Archie's, heading for the front door. She was going to escape!

***

Detective Edwards and Officer McCoy cautiously approached the hallway, tasers drawn. The man with the shaggy red hair jumped out of a closet, swinging a crowbar. Officer McCoy

100

The Haunted Mansion

ducked under the blow and tackled the man to the floor, sending the crowbar flying.

The tall thief in the black hoodie stood defiantly in the hallway. He brandished the wand of the plasma cutter, flames shooting out the end like a six-inch, fiery blue knife. His pale, olive-green eyes stared at Detective Edwards, unblinking, fearless.

"Put the torch down," demanded Detective Edwards. "This isn't going to end well for you."

"What?" the man asked, as if confused. "This thing?"

He raised the flaming wand to the ceiling, triggering the sprinkler system. Instantly, a powerful jet of water sprayed into Detective Edwards's face, momentarily blinding him. The thief rushed forward, dropping his shoulder into the detective's chest, driving him to the ground.

Detective Edwards groaned and rolled to his side as the thief raced back toward the tunnel. "Norris!" he gasped into his radio. "He's coming!"

***

Water poured from the ceiling; emergency strobe lights flashed. The woman with the shaved head burst through the doorway and slid into the reading room. Ava pulled her soaking-wet, matted hair from her face and peered around the edge of the couch. She watched in horror. The woman was going to get away!

101

"The couch!" whispered Ava to Derik and Carol. "Hit her with the couch!"

The woman crashed into the front door. She gripped the slippery doorknob and then, to her surprise, she was suddenly airborne, as the trio slammed the couch into her like a battering ram. She landed hard, skidding across the floor.

"Got her!" yelled Ava. But her excitement was short-lived. The woman leapt to her feet, glaring at them.

"Out of my way, or I'm going to snap your necks," snarled the woman.

"That's not good," gulped Carol. "She's like a super ninja."

"You don't scare us!" yelled Ava.

"Speak for yourself," said Derik. "I personally find her terrify—"

Derik didn't get to finish his sentence as the woman steamrolled over him. Using his chest as a springboard, she jumped up and over the couch. She slammed the bolt lock open with the palm of her hand and grabbed the doorknob.

"Oh, no, you don't!" screamed Carol like a wild banshee.

She jumped onto the couch and launched herself onto the woman's back.

"I'm coming," yelled Ava, slipping and sliding around the sofa. She closed her eyes and dove at the woman's legs. To her surprise, the woman didn't fall. However, she did find herself wrapped around the woman's leg like a monkey.

"Get off me!" yelled the woman, kicking violently while simultaneously slamming Carol against the wall.

"Not gonna happen!" yelled Ava, imagining herself as a rodeo rider. The woman was incredibly strong. Ava was beginning to wonder how much longer she could hang on, when she heard Derik's beautiful voice cry out, "Face...plant!"

Suddenly, the woman groaned and toppled to the floor. The girls looked up to see Derik smiling, holding a broken flowerpot in his hand.

"Get it?" he smiled. "Face...plant."

The woman moaned as the trio sat on her back. Officer Davis rushed into the room, slipping and sliding.

"Boom! Ride's over, crazy lady," said Ava to the woman, pretending to drop a microphone.

Officer Davis stared in amazement at the woman moaning on the floor, her head covered with mud and flowers. "You guys okay?" she asked, trying not to laugh.

"We're fine," smiled Carol. "The plant," she said, pointing to the broken pot, "not so much."

***

Detective Edwards turned the corner just in time to see the blond-haired thief lower himself through the grate. Seconds later, he heard a loud electrical zap. He winced, knowing that the man had run right into Lieutenant Norris and his taser.

Wiping the water from his eyes, he made his way back to the hallway. Officer McCoy had just handcuffed the thief with the shaggy hair. He turned and gave Detective Edwards a thumbs-up.

***

The sprinkler system and flashing strobes had finally shut off.

"This is horrible," said Carol, looking around at the destruction. *Hopefully, his most valuable items are in the safe or in display cases.*

A blinking red light flashed in the front window of Archie's, catching Ava's attention. She glanced up, just in time to see a black drone fly away. Running to the door, she flung it open and stepped out into the street. A tall thin man jumped into a sleek black car, but not before Ava recognized him: Harvey from the Public Works Department.

"Carol!" yelled Ava. "Wardrobe!"

18
MAY THE FORCE BE WITH YOU

The trio ran through Archie's into a room filled with display cases containing costumes from famous movies.

"Grab a costume and get changed! We've got to hurry," yelled Ava.

Carol flung a vintage Captain America costume to Derik. "Change into this," she said, pushing him out the door.

Ava scanned the display cases. *Wonder Woman...no. Batgirl...no.* She needed something warm and mobile, and that's when she saw it. Gumby!

Carol peeled off her clothes and began pulling herself into a furry Chewbacca costume.

Moments later, Derik rapped on the door dressed as Captain America. He quickly crossed the room and grabbed a red, white, and blue scooter with a large white star.

"You know what to do, right?" asked Carol, narrowing her eyes.

"Trust me, I'm on it!" said Derik, nodding.

"Godspeed, Winter Soldier," said Ava, as Derik ran to the front door and zipped away on the scooter.

"Ava? Carol? What the heck are you doing?" asked Detective Edwards, a confused look on his face.

"We're catching the drone pilot—it's Harvey, from public works," said Ava, putting on a large pair of green foam boots.

"Tell Officer Tiny to meet us at Crispin Pond!" said Carol. "We won't do anything until he gets there!"

"If he sees you, he'll disappear," said Ava. "He's got a tunnel system with tons of secret exits, two cars…please, Blake!"

"We promise we'll hide in the woods until Officer Tiny gets there. I have a plan," said Carol.

"Time is *not* on our side right now," said Ava. "We know what we're doing."

Detective Edwards shook his head and exhaled. "I'm going to regret this, aren't I?"

"If he gets away," said Ava, "then, yes. We're blaming it all on you."

"Okay. Wait for Officer Tiny before you do *anything*!"

"Yes, sir," said Carol, putting on her Chewbacca mask.

"May the force be with you," laughed Officer Davis, shaking her head.

19
DERIK SEES BLUE

Ava and Carol crouched behind a clump of snow-covered evergreen trees, at the edge of what was once Crispin Pond. A chill ran through Ava's body, making her shudder.

"I should have picked a warmer costume," she whispered, wrapping her arms around her body.

"Yeah, mine's quite toasty," replied Carol. "Do you think we made it in time?"

"I don't see any fresh tire tracks," said Ava, pointing at the pristine, freshly fallen snow.

"My question is, where the heck is Derik? He had a huge head start on us," said Ava.

"I know," said Carol, grabbing her phone. "He was supposed to text us when he got here."

"Maybe he's in trouble," said Ava.

"Harvey could have kidnapped him, or worse!" whispered Carol.

Ava looked at Carol. "Are you thinking what I'm thinking?"

"I never thought I would say this," said Carol, dropping her head, "but most likely...yes."

Without another word, the girls crept across the icy ravine, crouching behind the huge rock wall that hid the thieves' car. Ava crawled on her hands and knees and peeked her head around the corner. The thieves' old gray Toyota was still there!

"Derik!" she hissed, holding her foamy green hand to her mouth. "Derik, are you there?" Nothing.

She crawled back to Carol and shook her head. "The thieves' car is still there, but there's no sign of Derik."

"I'll try texting him," whispered Carol, fearing the worst.

Carol had just grabbed her phone when they heard footsteps crunching in the snow. Ava crawled on her belly, peering around the edge of the rock. A tall, thin man with a goatee and ponytail was struggling under the weight of two black duffle bags.

She slid back behind the rock. "It's Harvey," she hissed. "He's got two heavy duffel bags!"

"The money and the jewels," whispered Carol. "Did you see Derik?"

Ava frowned and shook her head. "No," she whispered.

The sound of the trunk slamming made the girls jump.

"We can't wait for Officer Tiny—Harvey's going to get away!" said Carol.

"You're right," replied Ava, leaping to her feet.

"Ava, what are you doing?!" hissed Carol.

"Come on, I've got a plan!"

"Wait," said Carol, grabbing Ava by the elbow. "What's the plan?"

"I'm making it up as I go along!" yelled Ava as she dashed around the rock wall.

Harvey opened the car door and had one leg in the car when Ava shouted, "Harvey! Harvey Cooper!"

Harvey whirled around to face the girls. He shook his head and rubbed his eyes. Was that really Gumby and Chewbacca?

"Who are you?" he yelled. "What do you want?"

"We know what you did, Harvey. We know you stole the money. We know everything about you!"

"Oh, it's you two. I'll send you a postcard from Mexico," he laughed as he climbed in the car and slammed the door.

Carol and Ava jumped aside, expecting him to roar away, but the car didn't move. They could see Harvey beating the steering wheel and screaming. Then, as if it were a dream, Derik appeared from behind a rock. He marched up to the hood of the car, a fistful of wires dangling from his hand.

Carol punched Ava in the shoulder. "Look! He ripped out…." She shook her head, not knowing what to say. "He ripped out a bunch of important-looking wires!"

Enraged, Harvey kicked open his car door. Derik's eyes flew open wide as he ran screaming, hiding behind a pile of rocks. Harvey turned and stared evilly at the girls.

"You're gonna pay for this!" he screamed, racing toward the girls.

"Don't you have a plane to catch?" yelled Ava, trying to run in her Gumby costume.

Harvey grabbed Ava by the back of her foam head, pulling her toward the car, her feet dragging across the snow.

"Unhand her!" yelled Derik from atop a huge boulder, brandishing his Captain America shield.

Ava kicked and twisted, but Harvey held on tight. Just as he reached into his jacket for the car keys, Derik let out a ferocious scream. "Fly!" he shouted as he hurled the shield at Harvey.

Unfortunately, the shield weighed about twenty pounds. It flew about three feet and then sank into the snow. Even more unfortunate, Derik slipped from the huge boulder, crashing to the ground face first with a loud *oomph*.

He lifted his head and whispered "blue lights," and then collapsed back into the snow.

Harvey, momentarily distracted, screamed as Carol whipped a snowball directly into his face. Ava threw herself backward into him, knocking him onto the car's trunk. Just as he sat up, she hurled another snowball into his face.

A terrifying look filled Harvey's eyes, making Carol gulp.

"No more games," he growled. Keeping an eye on the girls, he opened the trunk of the car and pulled out a tire iron. "You couldn't leave well enough alone, could you?"

Ava looked at Carol; there was no way they were going to outrun Harvey.

"Follow me," whispered Ava. "I got a plan."

Ava bolted toward Derik with Carol right on her heels. Dropping to her knees she slid and grabbed the Captain America shield. Just as she put her arm through the shield's handle, Harvey took a wild swing at her with the tire iron hitting the shield.

The vibration from the blow sent a shockwave from her arm to her feet. Ava shook her head; it felt like her entire body was vibrating. She had just recovered when Harvey swung again—this time at her side. She dropped the shield to her side; the sound was deafening. The force knocked her to her knees.

"I think I broke my face," whispered Derik, "and my ankle."

"It's okay, buddy," said Carol, whipping another snowball into Harvey's face.

Harvey turned toward Carol and raised the tire iron. "You little—"

Bwong! Harvey's eyes rolled back in his head as Ava smashed the metal shield into his shins. He made a weird groaning noise as he fell to the snow, grabbing his lower legs. Carol rushed forward and grabbed the tire iron, while Ava approached from the other side, holding the shield.

"Game's over, Harvey," smiled Ava.

In the distance, the girls could see a mountain of a man rushing toward them, tufts of smoke billowing above his head like a steam engine. It was Officer Tiny.

"Better late than never," winked Carol.

Ava nodded, smiling.

"You girls all right?" he asked, gasping for breath.

"Yes, sir!" smiled Ava. "We present to you: one criminal," she said, pointing her shield at Harvey, "officially gift wrapped."

"The only thing he's missing is the bow," smiled Carol.

Harvey's head hung on his chest. In the distance, a snowmobile appeared over the ridge of the ravine, speeding toward them. A blue light flashing on the front.

"Blue light," whispered Derik, pointing at the snowmobile.

"That's right," smiled Carol as she helped him sit up. "Blue light."

"Is he okay?" asked Officer Tiny as he handcuffed Harvey.

"I think he may have broken his ankle," said Carol.

"And my face," mumbled Derik.

"And his face too," nodded Carol, gently brushing the snow off his Captain America mask.

Detective Edwards and Officer Davis roared up on a red snowmobile, sliding to a stop beside the old Toyota.

"Ava," called out Detective Edwards, leaping from the snowmobile. "You guys okay?"

"Better than him," said Ava, pointing at Harvey. "We seriously messed up his vacation plans."

"Derik may have a broken foot and a horribly bruised ego," Carol added.

"Officer Davis, if you could...," Detective Edwards prompted.

"I'm on it, sir," she called out as she hurried over to Carol to help her with Derik. "We'll get you over to Emerson ASAP, Mr. America."

"Captain," groaned Derik, smiling, "it's Captain."

"Lieutenant Norris is on the way to the Butcher house right now to see if his team can locate the stolen goods," said Detective Edwards.

"Yeah, about that...I'm sorry, but...I'm afraid the stolen goods aren't there anymore," said Ava, putting on her saddest face.

"What?" said Detective Edwards, instantly serious. "Are you sure?"

Ava nodded. "They were sending the stolen goods out of the country. But...if you were to open that trunk...," she smiled, pointing at the Toyota.

A huge smile filled Detective Edwards's face. "Ava Clarke, I don't know what I'm going to do with you."

Officer Tiny tossed Detective Edwards a set of keys. The detective looked at the keys for a second and then handed them to Ava.

"Here, you do the honors."

Ava turned and tossed the keys to Carol. "This was all Carol's plan," smiled Ava. "This is her moment."

"Thanks, Aves!" said Carol, taking the keys.

She unlocked the trunk, and then, struggling, placed the heavy bags on the ground in front of her. Everyone gathered around her as she unzipped the first duffel bag. There was an audible gasp from the group. The first bag was filled to the top with bundles of hundred-dollar bills.

"The bank's money," she whispered giddily.

She pulled the next bag closer and unzipped it. "Whoa," she whispered as hundreds of diamonds sparkled like stars in the moonlight.

Carol looked up and smiled at the group gathered around her. It was going to be a happy Christmas after all.

20

NOT AGAIN

It was the night before Christmas. A giant white moon hung in the sky. Wispy dark clouds, like pulled taffy, raced across the sky. In the darkness of the forest, evil lurked!

Ethan shivered and looked at his phone. *Where is he?* he wondered.

He had received an urgent text from Kevin Chen: *Meet me at the Butcher house! There's something you've got to see!*

Ethan stood at the top of the driveway. There was no way he was going any closer to that creepy old house alone. He pulled off a glove and held it in his teeth while he texted Kevin: *Where are you?!* He whirled around. *What was that?* Did he hear a stick snap? "Kevin, is that you?" he yelled out, his voice shaking more than he would like.

A light flashed on in the Butcher house. Ethan crouched down behind a small brick column at the end of the drive. He dared to sneak a look—it was an old man, standing at the window staring directly at him!

Suddenly, there was a scream and a loud thrashing in the woods. He stood to run, but his feet wouldn't move. There was another scream, and then Carol appeared! Her jacket and pants were ripped; she was trying to run, but it looked like her leg was injured. "Help! Help!" she cried out, falling into the snow.

Then Ethan saw it. His breath caught in his throat. It was a headless monster! A shrill, mind-numbing scream escaped Ethan's mouth. The headless monster turned toward him. Ethan's feet felt like lead, like in a dream when you can't run.

"No! No! No!" shrieked Ethan, backpedaling as the monster drew closer. He closed his eyes and stepped backward, tripping over a tree branch, falling hard onto his back. "No!" he screamed, crossing his arms across his face.

"And...end scene—that's a wrap, guys," called out Ava.

"What...what's going on?" asked Ethan, sitting up, completely confused.

"First," said Ava, moving her phone from person to person, "I'd like to thank Carol for playing the scared kid. You were brilliant," Ava smiled.

"Thank you," said Carol, bowing.

"Kevin...masterful," praised Ava. "That's all I can say."

"I felt like I was one with the monster," he smiled.

"It showed," laughed Carol. "Truly, a moving performance."

Derik hobbled up the driveway toward the group, his foot in a cast. "Derik, you did a phenomenal job as the old man."

"Thank you," smiled Derik, holding up a rubber mask.

"And lastly," said Ava, whirling back to Ethan, "I would like to thank you for your role as the frightened bully. You were flawless. Well, that ends our holiday production—time for the wrap party," laughed Ava.

"What the heck was this all about?" yelled Ethan, angrily jumping to his feet.

"We knew how much you like frightening people. We thought, in the spirit of giving, we'd scare you a little," said Carol.

"I wasn't scared," sneered Ethan, laughing

"Oh, interesting," said Ava, swiping her finger across her phone. The group literally jumped when she hit play—Ethan's scream was so shrill.

"I'm not sure," laughed Carol, "but I believe you shattered a few windows."

"Okay, okay, you got me," he smiled. "Fair's fair."

"Now, we're willing to forget all of this in the spirit of Christmas…if you promise not to scare the life out of the little children next year," said Ava, crossing her arms.

Ethan looked at the group, and then at Ava's phone.

"Not even a little?" he asked.

The group looked at each other and smiled. "Hey, we're not scrooges," smiled Derik. "We're talking about within reason."

117

"Okay, I promise. I promise only to scare children within reason," said Ethan, holding up his hands in surrender.

"Okay, that's that. Moving on," smiled Ava. "My mom's catering the wrap party at my house. Steaming-hot cocoa, and her famous homemade sugar cookies."

"You had me at sugar," smiled Derik.

Carol turned, looked at the Butcher house, and smiled; they had turned a horrible story into a positive one. They had captured the thieves and found the money and the diamonds. She threw her arms over Ava and Derik's shoulders and began belting out "We Wish You a Merry Christmas."

The group laughed and sang at the top of their lungs. It was a perfect night. As they arrived at Ava's house, Ethan gathered everyone into a close circle.

"Thank you, guys, for being so cool. And one other thing," he leaned in and whispered, "you guys wanna hear a scary story?"

We hope that you enjoyed reading The Haunted Mansion. Be sure to check out our other exciting books in the action-packed Ava and Carol Detective Agency series. Upcoming titles:

If you enjoyed the book, please leave a review on Amazon, Goodreads, or Barnes & Noble. We'd love to hear from you! Thank you so much for your help, we are incredibly grateful!

Learn about new book releases at avaandcarol.com

Others by Thomas Lockhaven

Printed in Great
Britain
by Amazon